ONLY THE BRAVE TRY BALLET

BY
STEFANIE LONDON

MILLS & BOON

Published in Great Britain 2014
by Mills & Boon, an imprint of Harlequin (UK) Limited,
Eton House, 18-24 Paradise Road, Richmond, Surrey, TW9 1SR

© 2014 Stefanie Little

ISBN: 978 0 263 91142 8

Printed and bound in Spain
by Blackprint CPI, Barcelona

Stefanie London comes from a family of women who love to read. When she was growing up her favourite activity was going shopping with her nan during school holidays, when she would sit on the floor of the bookstore with her little sister and painstakingly select the books to spend her allowance on. Thankfully, Nan was a very patient woman.

Thus it was no surprise when Stefanie ended up being the sort of student who would read her English books before the semester started. After sneaking several literature subjects into her 'very practical' business degree, she got a job in Communications. When writing emails and newsletters didn't fulfil her creative urges she turned to fiction, and was finally able to write the stories that kept her mind busy at night.

Now she lives in Melbourne, with her very own hero and enough books to sink a ship. She frequently indulges in her passions for good coffee, French perfume, high heels and zombie movies. During the day she uses lots of words like 'synergy' and 'strategy'. At night she writes sexy, contemporary romance stories and tries not to spend too much time shopping online and watching baby animal videos on YouTube.

**This is Stefanie London's first book for Modern Tempted™
and is also available in eBook format
from www.millsandboon.co.uk**

To Nan and Nonno for teaching me
what it means to be brave.

To my amazing husband for his endless supply of love
and support (and for always doing the dishes
when I was stuck in the revision cave).

To my family for never thinking my dreams
were crazy, or loving me enough not to say so.

To my editor, Flo, for seeing past the rough edges of
my first submission and taking a chance on this story.

CHAPTER ONE

WHAT DO A ballerina and a football player have in common? It was the question Jasmine Bell pondered as she watched the footballer in front of her struggling to master a *plié*. Discounting a need for flexible hamstrings... they have nothing in common. Absolutely nothing. Yet here they were.

She stood in the middle of the studio, wearing her usual uniform of a black leotard, tights and ballet shoes. These items were like a second skin to a dancer, but tonight she couldn't have felt more exposed than if she were standing there butt-naked. She folded her arms tight across her chest.

'Let's take it from the top. Keep those shoulders down,' she said, forcing a calming breath. She loosened her shoulders, rounded her arms into first position and turned her feet out to match. 'Prepare...left hand on the *barre* and *plié*—one, two, three, four...'

The man in front of her smirked as he followed her instructions with a lazy swagger. Everything about Grant Farley got under her skin, from the cocky grin on his face to the way his thick blond brows rose at her when she spoke. He was a man designed to destroy a woman's concentration.

Keeping her distance, she watched his movements and provided assistance verbally. Usually she helped her students by guiding them with her hands, but there was something about him that made her mind scream *Look but don't touch*. Maybe it was because he moved with a self-assurance that she envied, or maybe it was because after her six months of celibacy he looked good enough to eat.

Much to her chagrin he was a quick learner, and rapidly gained ground despite his insistence on goofing around.

'You're doing well,' Jasmine said as they paused between repetitions. She was determined to be the consummate professional, even if it was harder to pull off than the *pas de deux* from *Don Quixote,* Act Three. 'I can see improvements already and it's only your first lesson.'

'It's not exactly difficult,' he responded, his blue eyes meeting hers and sending a chill down her spine. His tone dismissed her praise. 'I'm bending up and down on the spot. A two-year-old could master that.'

Jasmine bristled. Only a beef-head Aussie Rules footballer would fail to see the importance of the step she'd taught him.

She pursed her lips. 'That's an over-simplification, don't you think?'

'Not really.' He crossed his arms and leant back against the *barre,* appraising her. 'You can give it a fancy French name if you want, but it's just bending your knees.'

'Well, I never thought a career could be made out of chasing a little red ball.' She tilted her chin up at him. 'But there you go.'

'Our balls *aren't* little,' he drawled, a smile tugging at the corners of his lips.

Her cheeks flamed. She ignored the innuendo and started the music, preparing herself to repeat the exercise facing him.

'Once more from the top.'

As the music started he followed her lead, bending with his feet in first position. The teacher in her couldn't ignore the fault of his technique, as he bent his hips moved out of alignment and his feet rolled inwards. She instinctively reached out to correct the error but retracted her hand when her brain kicked into gear.

'I don't bite.'

His wolfish grin seemed at odds with the promise of safety, but Jasmine wasn't going to let some arrogant joker mess with her head. *She* was the teacher; *she* was the one in charge here.

'You need to keep your hips steady.' She stepped forwards and placed a hand on each hip. His muscles were tight and flame-hot beneath her palms. He bent down into *plié* once more and she guided him, ignoring the frisson of electricity that shot through her.

'Make sure your core is pulled in. It will increase balance and stop you rocking forwards.'

'Like this?' He grabbed her hand and placed her palm against his stomach. She could feel the ripple of each muscle through his T-shirt. His sports tights moulded every curve of his muscle, every bulge...

Jasmine gulped, her blood pounding as though she'd run a marathon. *Get it together.*

'Yes, like that.' She withdrew her hand, the heat of him still burning her fingertips.

She was going to strangle Elise, her soon to be former best friend, for roping her into this disaster waiting to happen. She was going to—

'Earth to Bun-Head.' Grant waved a hand in front of her face, chuckling when she returned her focus to him. 'I don't see how this is helping my hamstring. Shouldn't we be stretching or something? We need to speed up this flexibility thing. I've got an important game coming up.'

He shook his leg and rubbed at the muscle.

'Flexibility is a slow process. You can't turn up to one ballet lesson and expect to be a contortionist. It takes time.'

'I'd settle for being injury-free,' he replied. 'But if you want to show me how you can put your ankles behind your head then be my guest.'

'This is *not* Cirque du Soleil.' Jasmine bit each word out through gritted teeth.

'It might as well be.' He checked the clock above them. 'Though, shocking as it might seem, I'm not here for the laughs. I want to fix my hamstring and get back to spending my time on *real* training.'

Jasmine wasn't ready to let him have the last word. Sure, she had her motivations for agreeing to take Grant on as a student, but that didn't give him licence to be rude. 'I'm not exactly here for enjoyment either.'

'If you loosened up you might find some aspects of it enjoyable.'

She sucked in a breath and willed herself not to respond. Glancing at the clock, she held in a sigh of relief as the hand neared 8:00 p.m. Their hour together had hardly been successful. In fact she could chalk it up as her most frustrating lesson ever…and this was only the beginning.

'Is it that time already?'

His amused tone set fire to Jasmine's resolve to play cool, calm and collected. She wanted to slap the mocking look right off his ruggedly handsome face. He raised an eyebrow, as if to punctuate his question.

This was going to be her life two nights a week for the next six months, and she wasn't looking forward to it one bit! Unfortunately these lessons weren't about the ideal way to spend her free time. No, it all came down to dollars and cents. Once again she was in a position where she needed to play up to some arrogant guy who thought he owned the world to be able to pay her bills.

'I think we can *finally* call it a night,' she said.

'Don't sound *too* upset to be rid of me.' He uncrossed

his arms and leant forwards, his broad shoulders casting a shadow over her.

'The lessons are for one hour, Mr Farley.' Her voice was tight and her lungs were arid and devoid of air. 'If you want more time you'll have to arrange it with the studio owner.'

'One hour is plenty, *Ms* Bell,' he teased, and raked a hand through his thick blond hair.

Why did he have to be so damn attractive? Her insides flipped as his hair sprang back into place. She headed towards the door to the waiting room and he walked with her, a little too close for comfort. The scent of his aftershave found its way to her nostrils and filled her head with unwanted though not unpleasant images. She shut her eyes for a moment, pushing away the desire that flared like the lighting of a match.

He wasn't good-looking in the traditional, clean-cut way she preferred. But there was something about his rough-around-the-edges look that drew her in. He had a strong jaw and razor-sharp cheekbones; his nose was crooked, as though it had been broken at some point and hadn't healed properly. She had a strange, powerful urge to run her fingertips over the bump, to confirm her suspicions.

She bit down on her lip. There was no way in hell she would let herself fall for a guy like him. Egotistical, cocky guys were a thing of her past, and she intended to keep it that way. It was strictly business, and after he paid her for the lesson she could go home and forget she was selling out. Forget that her dream had been reduced to this BS.

Grant walked over to his duffel bag and rifled through it, withdrawing a thick envelope. He thrust it in her direction.

'This should cover me,' he said. 'Coach thought it'd be easier to pay up front since you only take cash.'

The rewarding heaviness of the envelope sat in Jasmine's hands. It would cover her rent and bills for the next month or two, and give her a little breathing space. Relief coursed through her, immediately followed by a wave of shame as she tucked the envelope into her handbag. She didn't bother to count it. A guy who earned more than a million a year, if you believed the papers, was hardly likely to scrimp on a couple of hundred dollars for ballet lessons.

'Thanks,' she muttered without looking at him, dropping onto one of the couches and peeling off her leg warmers.

'Just so we're clear, this is something I have to do to tick a box. I don't have any secret dreams of wearing a tutu and getting up on stage. So don't take it personally if I don't crave your feedback.'

Self-important, arrogant, egotistical...

'Fine.' Untying her ballet shoes, she reached for her fleece-lined black leather boots. Her body was cooling down and her ankle ached. Grimacing, Jasmine rubbed at the soreness, feeling the rippled skin of her scar underneath her tights before sliding the boot on. 'You're here to tick a box. I'm here for the money.'

If he wanted to play it like that, then he could expect an equal response from her. Hopefully the weeks would pass quickly and then she could move on to figuring out what to do with her life.

As he pulled a pair of tracksuit pants from his bag Grant's leg muscles flexed and bulged through his leave-nothing-to-the-imagination sports tights. She'd spent the whole hour forcing her eyes up and away from the tight fabric that stretched over his thighs and...well, everything.

Heat crawled up the back of her neck and pooled in her cheeks. She pulled her eyes away as he stood and turned to her, staring at the ground as she pulled on her boots.

'See something you like?' he asked, his smile indicating it was a rhetorical question.

Dammit.

* * *

He regretted the words as they came out of his mouth, but Jasmine Bell stirred something in him that made him want to bait her. She had this prickly demeanour that he found both frustrating and fascinating.

He was used to swatting the football groupies away with a metaphorical stick. But Jasmine…well, she was a different breed entirely. All long limbs and straight lines, she was sexy as hell in spite of her don't-mess-with-me attitude. Or maybe that was *exactly* what he liked about her.

She glared at him as though she were mentally setting his head on fire. Her slender arms were crossed in front of her, as if trying to hide the lithe figure beneath. She wasn't going to give him the satisfaction of answering his question. There was a small part of him that enjoyed the power struggle; it was a game he liked to play. Moreover, it was a game he liked to win.

Now he'd ticked her off royally, and that was fine by him. He needed to keep his distance. Women were not a permanent fixture in his life…*people* were not a permanent fixture in his life. The fewer people he saw outside his footy team, the fewer people had the opportunity to use him. So he kept his distance, and he would do the same with her.

'Did becoming famous cause you to forget your manners, or is that the way you were raised?'

She smiled sweetly, her sarcastic expression stinging him as much as the intentional barb in her words. The tilt in her chin issued a challenge.

'All I wanted was to play footy; the fame is an unfortunate by-product,' he said, surprised by his own honesty. Her small rosebud mouth pursed, and her dark brows creased above a button nose. 'As are the ballet lessons.'

'Isn't that what they call a first-world problem?' She hoisted her bag over her shoulder and walked to the front door. He followed, holding back an amused smile. 'Like *Boo-hoo, I'm famous and it's such a tough life.*'

'I'd be happy to swap for a day so you can experience it first-hand.'

'As much as I'd love to see you in here, trying to wrangle a bunch of toddlers, you couldn't handle my job.' She held the door open for him, and offered another saccharine smile. 'Besides, I have the *most* annoying student to teach.'

Grant couldn't help it—a hearty laugh burst free. She was prickly, all right, but hot damn if he didn't enjoy it. 'Sucks to be you?'

He waited while she locked up, and then they walked to their respective cars. The lights on his Mercedes flashed as he pressed the unlock button. Inside the car was chilly, and the windows took a moment to clear.

By then Jasmine was gone. Within minutes Grant was zipping along the freeway, the street lights blurring orange outside his window as the car tore down the open road. It was late and the city had long cleared its peak hour congestion. He massaged his injured hamstring, the muscle aching under the pressure of his fingers.

Who would have thought something as prissy as ballet would be such a workout? Not that he would dare admit it to Jasmine *or* any of his team-mates.

His phone buzzed in the mobile-phone holder attached to his windscreen. The goofy face of fellow Victoria Harbour Jaguars player Dennis Porter flashed up. He swiped the answer button.

'Den.'

'How are the ballet lessons going?' Even through the phone line Dennis's mischievous tone was obvious. 'I wanted to see if your masculinity is slipping away by the minute.'

Ballet lessons were far from Grant's idea of fun, but a persistent hamstring injury meant the need for increased flexibility training, and who better to help with that than a ballerina? His physiotherapist had made it sound good in theory, but the reality was proving to be much more irritating—especially since it gave his team-mates more than enough fodder for locker room jokes.

'Ha!' Grant scoffed. 'Even if it was you wouldn't be in with a chance. You're not my type.'

'Yeah, yeah. That's what all the ladies say. So tell me that at least your teacher is hot?'

'*Hot* doesn't even begin to cover it.'

He'd been expecting someone older, more severe... maybe with a Russian accent. He'd had to keep his mouth firmly shut when a willowy beauty with a long black pony-tail and porcelain skin greeted him at the studio.

'Maybe I'll have to pop in to one of your lessons.'

A surprising jolt of emotion raced through Grant's veins at the thought of letting Den anywhere near Jasmine. He shook off the strange protective urge and forced his mind back to the present. 'I know you want to see me in action.'

'The whole country wants to see you in action. It's going to be a good season. I can feel it.'

'Me too.'

A drawn-out pause made Grant hold his breath.

'Do you think all that other stuff is behind you now?' Den asked.

Part of him wanted to answer truthfully. He didn't know if it would ever be behind him. How could you forget the moment you almost flushed your life's work down the toilet? Considering football was all he had, it was a damn scary thought. But Den was only a buddy, a mate...and as one of the more junior guys in the team he was not some-one to whom Grant could show weakness.

'Of course. You know me—I'm practically invincible.'

He hung up the phone and allowed his mind to drift back to Jasmine. She was a curious case, seemingly unaffected by him in the way other women were. How much did she know about his past? Was that why she eyed him with such wariness?

Regret coiled in his stomach. Gritting his teeth, Grant turned up the stereo and shook his head. The beat thundered in his chest and made his eardrums ache, yet he couldn't drown out the thoughts swimming like sharks in his head. Around and around they circled, occupying the space—scaring off any semblance of peace.

He slammed his palm against the sturdy leather-covered steering wheel. He wasn't looking forward to the rest of his ballet lessons, even with a teacher who was a walking fantasy. He had better things to do with his time…like figuring out how he was going to get his team to victory.

Given his not-too-distant fall from grace, he had a lot to prove and a reputation to rebuild. In particular he had to convince his coach, his team and the fans that he was at the top of his game again. The last thing he needed was to be distracted by a woman. If it were any other girl he'd simply scratch the itch and move on, but that wasn't going to be possible given the ongoing nature of their lessons.

Groaning, he pressed his head back against the headrest. He had a bad feeling about her; there was something about her that set his body alight in a way he hadn't felt for a long time. And the way she'd been staring at him after the lesson…talk about an invitation to sin. Warning bells were going off left, right and centre.

He couldn't do it—not now that he was finally making progress in clearing the mud from his name. This was going to be *his* season. Nothing was going to distract him; nothing was going to stand in his way.

'No!'

Grant sat bolt upright, rigid as though a steel rod had replaced his spine. Perspiration dripped down the side of his neck, his face, along the length of his spine. He felt around in the dark. The sweat-drenched sheets were bunched in his fists as he held on for dear life.

He was alone.

His breath shook; each gasp was fire in his lungs. His chest heaved as he sucked the air in greedily. More. More.

His eyes adjusted to the dark and he could make out the lines of the furniture around him. City light filtered through the slats of his blinds, creating a pattern on his bed. The apartment was silent; the rest of the world was sleeping while he shook.

Slowly his heartbeat resumed its normal rhythm. The tremors would take a while longer to go away—he knew that from experience. It was only a dream. *The* dream. The one he had over and over and over—the one that woke him with a fright every single time.

Flashbulbs disorientated him, microphones were shoved in his face.

'Grant! Grant! Is it true you put a man in hospital? Is it true you beat him to a pulp?'

Shaking his head, he disentangled himself from the bed-sheets and strode out to the living room. Starlight streamed in through the window and the city twinkled a silent tune. It was a surreal feeling to be in close proximity to thousands of people and yet be completely and utterly alone.

Opening the lid of his laptop, he settled onto the couch. His personal email showed the same sad scene it did every day: zero new messages. Even Dennis, the closest thing he had to a friend, hadn't sent him anything...not even a stupid Lolcats photo. He clicked on the folder marked 'family' and sighed at the measly three emails that he couldn't bear to delete. The last one was dated over six months ago.

He checked the spam folder, wondering if—hoping that—maybe a message had got caught in the filter, that maybe someone had reached out to him. No luck. The folder was empty.

He'd never regretted leaving the small country town where he'd grown up to pursue football and success in the big smoke, despite the verbal smack-down he'd got from his father. He could remember with clarity the vein bulging in his father's forehead as his voice boomed through their modest country property. Those three little words: *How could you?* How could he desert them? How could he abandon the family business? How could he put a pipe dream before his father and sister?

Those wounds had only started healing, with the tentative phone calls and texts increasing between him and his sister. The old bonds had been there, frayed and worn but not completely broken. Not completely beyond repair. Even his father had provided a gruff enquiry as to Grant's life in the city.

But all that was gone now. Those fragile threads of reconciliation had been ripped apart when he'd brought shame to the family name. They were his father's words but he couldn't dispute them. He didn't have the right to be mad. He was alone because of his own actions, because of the mess he'd made. And, knowing his father, he wouldn't get a second chance.

All the more reason to make sure the Jaguars were on top this year. If his career was all he had left he'd give it everything. He would *not* fail.

Slamming the lid of the laptop shut, he abandoned the couch to grab a drink from the fridge. If sleep was going to be elusive he might as well do something to pass the time.

CHAPTER TWO

'DAMMIT,' JASMINE MUTTERED as she battled with her large pink umbrella. The blustery weather meant it was virtually useless to ward off the sideways rain as it pelted her in the face and soaked her jeans.

Her hair streaked around her, the dark strands blocking her vision as she wrestled it into submission. She dashed across the busy street, feet sliding on the slick pavement. Panting, she hitched her bag up higher on her shoulder and ducked under the shelter of the doctor's clinic. She shook the umbrella, flicking droplets of water all around her, and walked through the automatic doors to the clinic's reception.

'Hi, Jasmine.' The receptionist greeted her with a familiar smile. 'Dr Wilson will be with you momentarily.'

Jasmine sank into a chair and wound her rain-drenched ponytail into a bun. Water dripped down the back of her neck and her ankle throbbed inside her boot, a constant reminder that the accident was not yet behind her.

Another one of the staff members gave her a friendly wave as they walked through the reception area. She was practically part of the furniture here.

After a brief check-up and lecture from her doctor Jasmine left, a fresh prescription in her hand since she'd fed the last one to her shredder. She hated taking the painkillers he'd prescribed; along with her inability to heal, they felt like another sign of weakness.

The doctor had again broached the topic of her seeing a psychologist...as though her problems were all in her head. But they weren't—they were real. Her ankle would never again be strong enough to sustain her *en pointe,* and without ballet she had nothing...*was* nothing. She wrapped her arms around herself as she made her way to the reception desk.

God she missed it—the glitter of stage lights reflecting off sequins, the thunder of the audience's applause, the thrill of mastering a new part. What could she do with her life now that all those things were gone? Every time she tried to think about it her mind went blank. There was nothing else in her heart except ballet, nothing else she was passionate about. It was ballet or bust...and she was definitely going bust.

Rain thundered outside the clinic and a bright flash lit up the windows, signalling that the storm was raging on. She regretted catching public transport; there was no way she'd get home dry. Stupidly, she'd come without the car she sometimes borrowed from Elise's mother, thinking perhaps she could save money if she stuck to buses and trams. In hindsight it was a doomed plan, given that Melbourne's public transport system was prone to failure when the weather turned. But without the cash for her own set of wheels she'd be rocking the drowned rat look on a more frequent basis.

Cursing, she signed the appointment form and paid with the notes from the envelope in her bag. It had her name scrawled across the front in Grant's chicken-scratch handwriting.

'Jasmine?'

A familiar voice demanded her attention. *Speak of the devil.*

Grant stood in the centre of the waiting room, dressed in his training gear. He looked infinitely more relaxed than the last time she'd seen him, his face open, though he hadn't lost any of the arrogance in his swagger. People in the clinic—mainly women—admired him openly and whispered to one another behind their hands.

'Fancy seeing you here.' She kept her voice professional, pushing aside the prickle of irritation left over from their first lesson together.

'The club gets remedial massage here.' He signed his own form with a scrawl. 'These tight calves are giving me hell.'

She couldn't stop the spread of an evil smile across her lips. Her calf exercises were notorious for punishing new students and she felt a small tingle of satisfaction that he was no different.

'Cry-baby,' she said, wrapping a fluffy orange scarf around her neck and preparing for the onslaught of the rain.

He chuckled. It was a sound designed to make a woman's stomach flutter, and hers did…right on cue. She cursed her body for its mindless response.

He walked beside her, and a frosty blast of air hit them as the automatic doors slid open to reveal a wet and miserable winter's day. 'What are you here for?'

'An old injury.' She paused under the awning of the clinic. She undid the clasp on her umbrella and opened it against the wind, wincing as the material flapped in protest. Turning to walk away from the car park, she waved. 'Well, I'd better run.'

Grant raised an eyebrow and cocked his head. 'You didn't drive?'

She couldn't blame him for thinking she was mad—even she was thinking she might have gone loopy. Who would choose to give up a car with seat warmers on a day like this? Her bones were already chilled to their core, and a five-minute walk to the bus stop was only going to make things worse.

She shook her head.

'I'll give you a lift. You can't walk in the rain.'

Grant set off towards the car park without waiting for her to accept his offer. She paused, her brows furrowing. Another blast of cold air made her shiver as she followed him. Indignation at his demanding tone wasn't going to force her to give up a free ride today.

Grant's long strides made quick work of the car park. He walked with his head bent to the wind, not looking to see if she'd followed him. She quickened her pace, her boots splashing through puddles as she jogged. The car's lights flashed as it was unlocked and Jasmine scampered around to the passenger side, eager to get out of the wet.

Slamming the door behind her, she shivered. Droplets of water had flicked all over the pristine leather seats, and the windows fogged from their breathing. Grant turned over the engine and flicked on the demister. They waited while the glass returned to its normal transparent state.

His eyes were on her.

Her pale skin was flushed from the cold. A strawberry colour stained her cheeks and, even as dishevelled and rain-soaked as she was, Jasmine was still the most stunning woman Grant had ever encountered.

'Where am I taking you?' He started the engine and let the car idle while it warmed up.

'To the ballet studio.' Blowing on her hands, she rubbed them together and shivered in her seat. 'Please.'

Grant turned up the heater, flicking the centre vent so that it blew in her direction. He could smell the combination of perfume and rain on her skin. Water droplets slid down her neck, disappearing beneath her scarf. For some reason he found that indescribably erotic.

'So you're dealing with an injury?' He forced his mind onto another topic. Injuries were safe, unsexy. 'From dancing?'

'Yeah.' Her voice sounded tight and she didn't elaborate.

He stole a glance at her profile as he turned to the rear window, easing the car out of its spot. She shot him a rueful smile, a dimple forming in her cheek. His eyes flickered over her small but full-lipped mouth.

'I bet you get more injuries in football, though—like a broken nose, perhaps?' Her voice held a slight sense of mischief.

Most girls wouldn't be so quick to point out that he had a crooked nose. But, then again, he could see she was different in every way from the women he met on the football circuit. She wasn't fake tanned and bleached to the hilt. She didn't have that artificial look that was the uniform of the WAGs. She was an authentic beauty—a rarity. Her long black hair was wound into a neat bun, and the only skin that showed was on her hands and face. She had a certain primness about her that Grant found appealing—a polished elegance that made her look every bit the perfect prima ballerina. And she gave him attitude left, right and centre.

'Yes to the broken nose, but it didn't happen on the footy field,' Grant said, returning his eyes to the front. 'I had a fight when I'd barely turned eighteen. It was my first night out drinking and I got into a fight at a bar.'

At one point that memory would have filled Grant with a sense of macho pride, as though it were a rite of passage for a young male. Now it made him queasy, with memories bubbling to the surface. Many women liked the whole 'bad boy' thing—hell, he'd used it to his advantage time and time again—but those days were well and truly over. Not that anyone believed him.

'That was a *long* time ago.'

He kept the mood light, but Jasmine wasn't letting him get away that easily.

'I don't understand why guys fight.' She shook her head. 'You don't need to beat your chest to attract the ladies, you know.'

'It wasn't like that.'

'What *was* it like?'

'I was young, thought I had to prove something.' He forced a hand through his hair. 'I wasn't always this way.'

'What do you mean?'

He was at a loss for words. People usually didn't ask personal questions—well, not those beyond what his bank balance was. They never showed any interest in him as a person, never cared about who he was…where he came from.

He shrugged, grappling for a response. 'In charge.'

'I have no doubt that you can take care of yourself,' she said, a soft smile on her lips. 'But being macho isn't the way to go about it.'

Perhaps she'd seen the media fuss that had erupted after the incident. There had been an awful paparazzi shot of him doing the rounds on the internet for months afterwards. Luckily the media moved on quickly. Sports stars behaving badly were a dime a dozen. Grant had experienced a sense of guilt when it died down so quickly, though the story still popped up on gossip sites whenever there was a slow news day.

'You don't get ahead in AFL by being a softy.'

'I don't know. I reckon you might be a big softy on the inside.' She laughed, poking him in the ribs. 'You're like one of those mean-looking dogs that rolls over for a tummy scratch.'

'I'm at the top of my profession, sweetheart.' He wanted to come across as controlled, but the words sounded hollow to his own ears. Defensive. 'I'm not in it for the belly scratches.'

'So what *are* you in it for?'

'I'm in it for the game.'

'You like to win?'

'Hell, yeah, I like to win.' He laughed. 'Don't you?'

'Depends on your definition of winning, I guess.'

A dark shadow passed over her face and for a moment he caught a glimpse of something beneath the surface of her warm brown eyes.

She moved on before he could probe deeper. 'Why weren't you always in charge?'

Of course she'd latched on to *that* little statement. Memories flickered at the edge of his consciousness. He didn't want to talk about this. He'd never told anyone about what he'd left behind, about the guilt that racked him for abandoning his family only a year after his mother had passed away.

'Let's just say I was a late bloomer.'

'And now?'

'Like I said, I'm at the top of my game.' His eyes flickered over to her. 'Belly scratches not required.'

There was no way she'd understand. Her face was neutral, giving nothing away. She kept her gaze trained on the front window, her hands folded primly in her lap.

'If you're at the top of your game then why are you concerned with my opinion?'

'What exactly *is* your opinion?' He steered the car around a corner and forced his eyes to stay on the road. He wanted to see her expression, watch for a hint of how she really felt.

Why did he even care?

'Like you said to me the other night—don't take it personally... I don't understand why football is such a big deal. I mean, you chase a ball around a field until someone kicks it between two posts. It's not rocket science.'

'We live the life of a dedicated athlete, we give up the things regular people take for granted.'

'I'm sure keeping up with the constant partying and bedding groupies is a *real* sacrifice.'

'Yeah, it's hard to keep up with the groupies, but I try my best.' He winked at her while they were stopped at a red light. 'It's good for building stamina.'

'You're unbelievable.' She rolled her eyes.

'So I've been told.'

Deflecting her away from the personal stuff with OTT arrogance wasn't his finest hour, but it had steered her away from the dark parts of him and it had made her laugh. As far as he was concerned it was a win.

She huffed and shook her head. Grant couldn't help but notice the pink flush that had spread from her cheeks down her neck, and she squirmed under his gaze.

He drove the car down the street that led to the ballet studio. Automatically he felt his shoulders tense as they drew closer. The feeling of dread that he experienced each time he came to the studio kicked in as he pulled into the car park. It was as if his body associated the studio with the pressure he was putting on himself—a manifestation of the fine line he walked with each game this season.

'Thanks for the lift.' Jasmine gathered her bag and umbrella from beneath her feet. 'That rain would have been awful to travel in.'

'No problem.' He tried to keep his eyes forwards, but he couldn't help stealing a glance as she stepped out of the car. The clingy fabric of her pants showed off one magnificently tight, toned ass. He gulped.

'See you tomorrow.'

Jasmine practically bounced from the car to the studio, her pink sports bag swinging against her hip while her pert behind wiggled enticingly. Grant gave himself a moment to let his breath settle before he peeled out of the car park.

Don't even think about it.

A quiet studio was not what Jasmine needed right now. The silence encouraged thinking, and sifting through the questions in her head was not productive…not when she had to focus on work. She stood at the *barre,* rolling her ankle around in a slow circle. The joint protested, the tendons tugging sharply as she pushed herself to flex or point a little more. If only she could push it a little farther each time…

Years of stretching had given her a perfect curve *en pointe,* but now she could barely rise up onto the balls of her feet. They refused to stretch, refused to flex and curve as they once had.

Gritting her teeth, she attempted a few moves from an old routine. Her feet thumped against the floor, clumsy in their poor imitation of how she had once danced. She wanted so badly to be able to go back to the way she'd been before the accident, before she'd stranded herself in this horrible place known as dancer's limbo—where you were too broken to move forwards, too proud to go backwards and too engrained to go anywhere else.

She missed dancing with an ache that felt as if it split her chest wide open every time she failed to flex her feet properly. There were times when she feared that her soul might wither up and die if she went much longer without dance.

Voices from the waiting room pulled her out of her dark thoughts; she whipped her head around.

Grant stood in the waiting room, talking to her best friend and owner of the studio, Elise Johnson, but his eyes were undeniably on Jasmine. Even from a distance she could see the fire burning in their ice-blue depths. He nodded in response to something Elise said but he didn't tear

his gaze from her…not even for a second. Stomach fluttering, she crossed the studio. Their muffled voices became
clearer as Jasmine reached the waiting room.

'How come your girlfriend doesn't come and watch
you practise?'

Elise batted her eyelashes at Grant as Jasmine poked
her head into the waiting room. She bit down on her lip
to stop herself from groaning; the girl was as subtle as a
sledgehammer.

'No girlfriend.' Grant shook his head, catching Jasmine's eye and winking.

'Wife?'

'Definitely not.'

'Interesting.' Elise cocked her head to one side and
smiled at Jasmine conspiratorially as she turned to grab
her coat and bag. 'Well, I'm off. Enjoy your lesson.'

Her smile was sweet as a cupcake piled high with frost-
ing. Jasmine stifled a laugh at Grant's get-me-out-of-here
expression. Elise was full-strength girlie—none of that
watered-down diet stuff. As Grant came forwards Elise
shot Jasmine a thumbs-up behind his back. Her face sparkled.

Despite the fact that Elise was single herself, she'd made
it her mission to try and set Jasmine up, no matter how
many times she protested.

She held open the door to the waiting room. 'Shall we
get lesson number two over with?'

'It's going to feel even longer if you count down every
single lesson,' Grant said, walking past her, close enough
that she could smell the faint aftershave on his skin.

'You were the one who wanted to speed up the results,'
she said, focusing her attention on the mirrored wall as
they walked over to the *barre*. Each breath had to be forced
in and out of her lungs, as though she might forget to
breathe if she were near him for too long.

'Do I need to wear these stupid things every lesson?' He pulled at the fabric of his sports tights and allowed it to snap against his thigh. 'At least at footy I can wear shorts over the top.'

'Are you worried about your modesty?' She raised an eyebrow.

'It's not *me* I'm worried about.'

She put on her most serious teacher voice. 'I need to see how your muscles work while we're going through the exercises.'

Heat crawled up her neck and she forced her eyes to stay on his face. She would not look down. She would *not* look down.

'My muscles? Right.' He drew the last word out, barely containing his laughter.

'I think you should consider taking these lessons a little more seriously, Grant. Preventing injury is no laughing manner.'

'God, you sound like an insurance commercial.'

He was pushing her on purpose, and he seemed to be getting an immense amount of pleasure out of it. Since this was *her* lesson, she could pay him back.

'Why don't we get started with some calf raises?'

He rolled his eyes and groaned, as though she'd told him he needed to climb a mountain with one hand.

'Suck it up, Grant. If there's one thing you should know about people who've studied ballet it's that we have discipline beyond anything you could imagine.' She sounded smug, sure, but he totally deserved it.

He shook his head and laughed. 'You're not selling the ballet ideal very well.'

'You don't think you've got what it takes?' She cursed herself. She shouldn't be baiting him. No doubt he'd be the kind of guy to enjoy a little verbal sparring. But the words

had slipped out before she could stop them. It was too…
fun. And she needed a little fun right now.

He grinned at her, confirming her fears. 'If I want something, there ain't a force in the world that will stop me
from having it.'

Jasmine gulped. His pointed look sent liquid fire
through her veins. There was no doubt in her mind that
she was on his list of things to want. She had to remind
herself that this was business and—fun as it might be, she
was only after a pay cheque. But that grin…the crooked,
self-assured way he smiled…it was like a fist through her
stomach.

No, this would *not* work on her. She wasn't another air-
head groupie, ready to fall at his feet.

'You can't have everything you want. That's not how
the world works.' And didn't she know it.

He raked his eyes over her. 'Watch me.'

Awareness tingled on her skin. She could feel his gaze
so keenly that it might as well have been the brush of his
fingertips or the rasp of his tongue for what it was doing
to her insides. She bit down on her lip, trying unsuccess-
fully to blank out the flickering reel of R-rated images in
her mind.

'Since you're so strong of mind, why don't you focus
some of that energy on this lesson?'

After Grant had made his way through the warm-up she
moved them on to a new exercise, facing him at the *barre*.

'We'll start the *tendu à terre* in first position. Watch
me.' She extended her right leg forwards until only the tips
of her pointed toes touched the ground.

Looking as out of place as one would expect from a
footballer in a ballet studio, Grant struck an angled ver-
sion of first position with his working arm, his shoulders
bunched up around his neck.

Jasmine rested her hand on the tense muscle. 'You

have to loosen up from here or you'll never relax into it,' she said, running her hands down his arm and shaping it into the proper position. Her fingertips brushed his hard, curved biceps. Her breath quickened while her heart bounded like an over-excited puppy. 'Now, extend your working leg forwards slowly. Point your foot and keep it on the ground.'

He shifted as he moved his leg forwards, tipping his hips out of alignment. Her hands automatically went down to put them back into place. Her fingers fluttered involuntarily against his hipbone. Through the thin fabric of his running tights his muscular thighs were perfectly visible. The fitted garment didn't leave much to the imagination... and, speaking of imagination, hers was running wild.

From the sharp intake of his breath and the flare of his pupils he must have felt it too. And the jolt of electricity that made her whole body feel like a live wire—could he feel that as well?

She stepped back and instructed him to complete the exercise on his own. Using her remote, she played classical music so he had timing to work with. He fought to keep his posture straight and Jasmine clasped her hands in front of her to stop herself from reaching out to touch him again.

'That's looking good. If we can get those hips to stay square, then you'll master this in no time. The *tendu* leads on to a lot of other steps in ballet.'

She was babbling—a side-effect from the onslaught of lust. God, it had been far too long since she'd been with a man, it must be the hormones making her crazy. That's all it was, a perfectly reasonable and natural response...absolutely nothing to do with him. She needed a break. Now.

'Why don't you grab a drink?' She walked to the front of the studio where her water bottle sat next to the MP3 player and her mobile phone. 'We'll get started again in a few minutes.'

They had another half an hour to go—how was she going to keep herself in check for that long? She took a swig of her water and relished the cool liquid sliding down the back of her throat.

'Did you ever think about going pro with your dancing?' His voice caught her off guard and she stiffened.

Busying herself with the MP3 player, she grappled for a response. She tried to swallow, her mouth suddenly dry.

'I'm not sure if any ballerinas would refer to it as "going pro."'

'Picking on my slang is an excellent way to avoid the question,' he said. 'But I'll rephrase. Did you ever think about dancing professionally?'

'Yes.' Not a lie, but not an invitation either.

'And?'

She bit her lip and sighed. The last thing she needed was for him to pity her…or, worse, want to help in some way. She always dealt with problems by herself; she preferred it that way. Dealing with things on her own meant there was no one pushing their ideas on her, no one convincing her to do something outside her comfort zone and no one controlling her.

But how could she get around this topic for the rest of their time together? At some point it would come up again and she'd have the same dilemma: lie or expose herself.

'I was a soloist with the Australian Ballet.' She kept her voice even, unemotional. 'I trained in ballet my whole life and have wanted to be a professional ballerina ever since I was eight years old.'

'Then why did you quit?'

'I didn't quit.' The word tasted dirty in her mouth. She would *never* have stopped dancing if her hand hadn't been forced. 'I was injured in a car accident and now I don't have full movement in my foot and ankle. I can't dance *en pointe* anymore.'

She opened her mouth to continue but the words died in her throat. Her lips were parched and her tongue was heavy, as if physically resisting the truth. She couldn't mention the constant pain. The mental torment. The shame of how it had happened.

She couldn't talk to anyone about that—not even her best friend.

Grant was silent, lines forming at the centre of his forehead. His thick brows were knitted together. Out of nowhere his left hand reached out and clasped hers. Jasmine jumped at the unexpected touch. Her hand was tiny in his grip. Fragile.

CHAPTER THREE

HE CLASPED THE fragility of her hand between his fingers, her bones feeling tiny and delicate and perfect. She gasped, her lips opening and closing, before she clenched her jaw. She'd been hurt before, and she wore it like a warning sign that read Stay the Hell Away.

She frowned, her rich brown eyes narrowing at him as she withdrew her hand from his grip. He wasn't even sure why he'd touched her, but something stirred deep within him. Everything about her was restrained, from her not-a-hair-out-of-place bun to her neatly filed pink fingernails. She had a carefully constructed veneer that held him at arm's length, and while he had no interest in getting closer she looked as though she could use the comfort. Yeah, he was comforting her...it had nothing to do with the strange ache in his chest.

'I'm sorry to hear that.'

'Not as sorry as I was.... You're here to work on your flexibility, remember?' Her voice wobbled slightly but she retained control. 'You're here to work.'

The way her eyes glittered and her cheeks were stained pink told him he'd unintentionally hit a nerve. How interesting. A woman with a mystery was his personal weakness, and there was a hell of a lot more to her story than she was letting on. He was drawn in by the opportunity to uncover her secrets, to peel away the layers of complexity that shrouded her. He would pick his moment, when she wasn't so raw, so exposed. He would find out what had hurt her more than a shattered dream.

'I mean it.' She walked towards him and stopped barely inches from where he stood. 'Back to work.'

The air between them sizzled. Grant's heart thudded an erratic beat in his chest. Her power seemed to come from nowhere. She'd frozen him on the spot with a single look. Her eyes blackened, pupils engulfing the ring of warm brown around it. She stood in front of him, close enough to touch. He could feel every damn millimetre between them and he wanted desperately to close the gap, to draw her to him with force.

But she was playing the same game he was. Testing the boundaries. Pushing to see how far they could go.

She returned to the *barre,* seemingly unperturbed. 'Let's keep working on your *tendu* for now.'

Jasmine settled her body into the starting position and waited while Grant did the same. She demonstrated where the turn-out should be coming from by touching the tops of her thighs where they connected to her hips, her hands inches from the place he wished his own hands were...or maybe his mouth.

Grant swallowed. She looked at him through her thick curly lashes as though she was completely aware of how difficult he was finding it not to stare. Damn her, she was doing it on purpose.

'Extend forwards.' She completed the move facing him, so that their feet met in the centre.

Her words counted out the beats of the music and he trained his eyes on her legs, making a poor imitation of her movements. He should leave her well alone, but something kept pulling him in. Something in the way she held him at arm's length made his blood pulse harder and hotter in his veins.

'Try again.'

She started the music—the same strains he'd listened to over and over that lesson. His feet moved in time, the steps less foreign to him now.

Neither of them spoke while he completed the exercise. She stood stock-still, observing him. There was something strangely sensual about the complete silence except for the whisper of their feet against the floor. The air crackled between them.

Her eyes flicked over his body. Was she assessing or admiring?

'You need to rotate your turn-out more,' she said, walking to him. She placed her hands on his upper thighs, smoothing the muscles outwards. 'Otherwise you're putting a lot of strain on the knees.'

Her hands lingered on his thighs, all too close to where his body cried out for her touch. He stirred and bit down on his lip. There was no way he'd be able to hide an erection in these damn tights.

At this distance he could see that her eyes were not merely brown but a medley of chocolate shades: milk, caramel and dark cocoa. Her skin was porcelain-white. She lacked the flaws—freckles and scars—that years on the field had given him. Her lips were rosebud-pink, parted and moistened by the gentle swipe of her tongue.

'If you leave your hands there I take no responsibility for what happens.' He leant in, closing the gap between them.

Her eyes flickered up to him, her lips pursing. God, he wanted to taste her. Was she game?

'Lucky for you I have no problem with taking responsibility,' she said, withdrawing her hands. 'You should try it some time.'

Damn.

As they cooled down and stretched out she kept her distance, eyeing him as one might a large dog that wasn't on a lead. He was momentarily distracted by the sharp pull in his hamstring. Stifling a groan, he leant into the stretch but couldn't get enough from it. This damn injury was affecting his game and it was pissing him off.

'Do you want a hand with that?' She pushed up onto her feet and came closer.

He waggled his eyebrows. 'Yeah, I want a hand—'

'Finish that sentence and you'll get nothing,' she warned.

Jasmine Bell wore the prissy schoolteacher look better than he'd thought possible.

He kept his mouth shut and she knelt down in front of him. 'Lie flat on your back and put your right leg up. I'll give you a little push.'

Was it his imagination or did a subtle flush of pink rise up her neck as she instructed him? She leant her shoulder into the back of his thigh and eased forwards. With her body too close to his, he should have been revelling in the fantasy.

Unfortunately the muscle was so resistant he had to blow out a long breath and focus his energy on allowing it to lengthen. For once he couldn't even voice the innuendo.

Cold fear trickled down the length of his spine. What if his injury couldn't be fixed? What if he couldn't lead the Jaguars to victory? He'd bet everything on his career, and if he lost he'd have nothing at all.

At the time of her next lesson with Grant, Jasmine was in the studio, choreographing a routine for the teachers of the EJ Ballet School. Looking sexy as hell in a leather jacket over his hoodie and jeans, he stood about in the waiting room, watching her through the viewing mirror. He was early...for once.

Instead of heading straight out, Jasmine had the sudden urge to put on a show. She stretched out at the *barre,* determined to show off the best of her flexibility. Inside, her head sensibly protested that he was not the kind of guy to encourage. But the thought that he might up the ante of their teasing sent a shiver down her spine. Their last lesson had thrown her into a spin. His questions, the genuine concern in his voice, the tenderness of his touch…it was enough to make even the most sensible girl fantasise. And *sensible* was Jasmine's middle name.

Her heart fluttered as she stretched, excitement dancing along her nerves. What was *wrong* with her? She shook her head and forced herself to focus. Abandoning the *barre,* she set her shoulders straight and drew a deep breath.

Elise got to Grant before Jasmine made it to the waiting room. She was throwing *all* her charm at him—flipping her wispy blond ponytail and offering him a smile that could power a small city. Something twisted in Jasmine's gut—a strange pang that she hadn't experienced in a long time. She pushed it aside and walked out in time to catch the tail-end of their conversation.

'That would be amazing!' Elise's voice was high-pitched. Buoyant. 'Did you hear that? Grant is going to get us access to the Long Room for Friday's game. We can watch him in action.'

A warm heat flared in Jasmine's chest. Access to the Long Room was more than a couple of general admin tickets. It was a sweet gesture, and for some strange reason it made her tummy flutter. Whether that was from the generosity of his act or the thought of seeing him in his element, she didn't know.

'Isn't that exciting?' Elise nudged Jasmine in the ribs with her elbow, a hint of warning in her voice.

'That's extremely generous,' Jasmine said.

However, as the warm flush of excitement faded she realised what his invitation meant. Access to the Long Room was kind of like an insider event in the art world—filled with people who knew one another, who dressed the same way, who belonged. And she didn't belong with the other halves of football's elite.

Her heart sank. 'Of course I'll have to make sure I don't have anything else on.'

'You *don't* have anything else on,' Elise said pointedly, her elbow once again digging into Jasmine's ribs. 'We'll definitely come and watch.'

Relax, she told herself, *it won't be like the art community. Sport is inclusive, right?* Her stomach pitched. Her ex had dragged her around to all manner of gallery openings, VIP exhibitions and artist previews. She'd never fitted in. Everyone at those events had been able to afford the art hanging on the walls. She'd had more in common with the paintings themselves than the people she'd been paraded in front of.

'Great.' Grant flashed them both a smile. His eyes lingered for longer than necessary on Jasmine. 'Elise has given me your number so I'll text you the details.'

'Great.' Jasmine fought to keep the sarcasm out of her voice. *Of course* Elise had given him her number—why would she expect anything less?

An amused smile played on his lips. The two women watched him walk into the studio, both of them locking on to the way his hips rolled in their lazy, sensual gait.

'I can't believe you gave him my number.' Jasmine glared at her friend as soon as the door swung closed behind him.

'I'm doing you a favour, Jazz,' Elise said, positioning her hands on her hips. 'He's drooling over you during class and you're too chicken to do anything about it.'

'That's *not* true. He's practically a celebrity—he could have any of those red-carpet bimbos by his side.'

'Yes, but he's looking at *you*.' Elise sighed. 'You're too blinded by your own stubbornness to see it.'

'I am not stubborn.' But even as she said it Jasmine knew it was a lie.

'Right.' As if on cue, Elise cocked her head and rolled her eyes. 'You know not every guy is like Kyle. Grant is different. He—'

'Stop it.' Jasmine shut her eyes. 'I don't want to hear any more.'

She loved Elise, but this was crossing the line. She didn't want anyone pushing her towards Grant—especially when she was having a hard time controlling herself around him as it was. There was something about him that drew her like a magnet.

Magnetic attraction or not, she knew a relationship with him would never work because she didn't belong in his world. She'd had her time in a glamorous community filled with extreme wealth, cliques and persistent paparazzi. She'd promised herself she'd never go there again. But something pulled her to Grant—something deep and inexplicable.

She watched him through the viewing window while he warmed up at the *barre*. Against her better judgement, she didn't look away.

The pre-game rush was what had drawn Grant into the world of football back in his childhood. Some guys lived for the relief that came when the siren sounded, others purely for the swell of the crowd's cheer upon victory. But Grant was all about the build-up, the anticipation…and this match had it in spades.

He told himself it was because the Jaguars were playing their fiercest rivals. But deep down he knew the jangling of his nerves was caused by two things: Jasmine, and the niggling sensation in his hamstring. He couldn't let it get the better of him today…not when so much was at stake.

'Bloody hell, you're a space cadet today.' A hand

slapped down onto his back, the sound barely registering above the locker room din.

'Huh?' Grant turned to see his team-mate, Archer, standing beside him, shaking his head. He was a small guy, as rovers tended to be, but he had a larger than life personality. His eyes glittered with mischief.

'You seem light on your feet lately, mate. I should start calling you Twinkle Toes.'

'Now, now...' their coach warned, his voice booming above the noise.

'I thought Grant might be able to share some of his experiences with the team.' Archer looked up at Grant, unperturbed by the half a foot height difference between them. 'How *are* the pirouettes going?'

'You don't want to go there, Arch.' Grant stretched up to his full height. 'Even doing ballet I'm still twice the man you are—mentally *and* physically.'

'Short jokes...clever.' Arch rolled his eyes as he stretched out his quad.

'Nothing wrong with getting in touch with your feminine side, is there Grant?' Another player chimed in.

'Back off.'

'Oh, don't be such a bad sport.' Arch elbowed Grant in the ribs. 'I'd say pink is your colour.'

'You're just jealous, Arch.' Grant felt the frustrations of the past year building, but he remembered the breathing exercises and calming techniques he'd learnt. Unclenching his fists, he let out a slow breath. 'I get one-on-one time with a hottie ballerina and you're going home to your old lady. I know who *I'd* rather be.'

Den Porter came up to the two guys and clapped them both on the back, chuckling at Grant's joke. 'Can't argue with that, can you, Arch?'

Archer muttered a retort but left Grant alone. The locker

room buzzed around them, pre-game jitters filling the air with a crackling, unpredictable energy.

'You *have* been a bit of a space cadet,' Den echoed, taking a long swig from his water bottle.

'I've got things on my mind.' Grant shrugged.

'They'd better be game-related things,' the coach said as he walked past. 'This season is your chance, Grant. An opportunity for redemption.'

'He sounds like a goddamn evangelist,' Grant muttered as the coach disappeared from earshot. 'He's got the memory of an elephant too.'

'Maybe you should have thought of that before you dragged the club into your personal life.' Archer's voice was stony. '*You* cost us that season.'

'If I remember rightly, you didn't score a single goal that game,' Grant said through gritted teeth.

'Who could concentrate, with you stumbling all over the place? You were a mess.'

Grant slammed his locker shut, enjoying the loud crack. He'd been on the straight and narrow for over six months now, but his team would never pass up the opportunity to have a go. They thought he'd cost them a winning season—their *first* winning season—and that his antics had distracted the team.

He'd given up the partying, he'd given up the booze, he'd even given up the groupies. But it wasn't enough; in everyone's mind *he* was the reason for their failure. He could still remember the last call he'd had with his father in the days after the story had hit the media. *'Now you're a deserter* and *a drunk. You're no son of mine.'*

'You whinge like an old woman, mate.' Den rolled his eyes at Arch.

The coach approached Grant, his weathered face drawn into a stony expression. 'Don't forget you promised me this season would be a winner, Farley. When I agreed to give you a second chance you told me you'd give me a winning season.'

'I will.'

'You'd better not have any distractions this time.' Two hard eyes bored into him. 'I make it a rule not to give third chances.'

Message received.

Jasmine and Elise arrived early to the Melbourne Cricket Ground, where all the big AFL games were held, to collect their tickets. As they were gaining access to the most exclusive part of the MCG they hadn't been able to dress down like the rest of the fans who were streaming into the stadium. Amidst the black-and-green Jaguar guernseys, and the occasional fan sporting the red and yellow of the away team, they looked out of place.

The winter air bit right through Jasmine's coat and boots, a fine mist of rain dampening her exposed neck. She shivered and huddled closer to Elise. They moved with the crowd, searching for the 'Members Only' area.

Following the signs, they eventually ended up in the Long Room, with its floor-to-ceiling views of the ground. It was another world. Away from the crowds and coloured flags of the general admission area. Away from the manic cheering, meat pies and scarf waving. Away from the 'real' football experience.

Up here men wore tailored suits and women dressed in all manner of finery, toting handbags that probably cost more than a month's rent. The sound of dramatic air kisses and tinkling laughter rose above quiet conversation.

'It's something else, isn't it?' Elise looked around, dazzled.

Jasmine shifted on the spot and removed her coat, slinging it over one arm. She smoothed her free hand down the front of the vibrant emerald dress she wore over thick black tights and boots. She'd changed a dozen times before leaving, even though she knew she was unlikely to see Grant after the game. Still, she'd fussed over endless combinations until she'd ended up back in the first outfit she'd tried on. Last minute, she'd thrown a long strand of onyx beads around her neck to try and fancy up what essentially was a plain cotton dress.

She looked even more out of place here than she had in the crowd. Elise loved being amongst the rich, but Jasmine hated it. Such wealth flung around, while she could barely scrape together enough money to keep her electricity turned on. She felt frumpy and juvenile next to these elegant swans in their silk dresses and needle-thin heels.

Worse, she'd been here before. The glitz and the glamour of the arts world wasn't so different—though there was a distinct lack of fake tan and fake boobs where ballet and art were concerned.

She'd been on the arm of a wealthy man—the son of a financier—who'd thought his family's bank balance meant that he owned her, that he could control her as he controlled the investments in his portfolio. His family had money equivalent to the GDP of a small nation.

And it had ended badly...*very* badly. Her stomach churned.

'Champagne, miss?' A waiter held out his silver tray, four delicate flutes of bubbling wine catching the light in front of her.

'No, thank you.'

'I will.' Elise reached for a flute and smiled.

The waiter drifted into the crowd and they found a spot to stand in front of the mammoth glass window. Outside the seats were filling up. A sea of black and green engulfed the stadium, and excitement was palpable in the atmosphere. Inside the clinking of champagne flutes and muted chatter filled the air.

'I would have thought you'd be OK to have a drink by now.' Elise took a delicate sip from her flute.

Her blond hair was piled on her head, with wispy strands loose and alluring around her pixie face. A chunky strand of grey pearls offset her steel-coloured eyes. Even Elise looked more as if she belonged than Jasmine did.

'It's not like I'm working hard to resist it,' Jasmine said.

'You're missing out—this is the good stuff.' She winked. 'The *French* stuff.'

'I don't want it.'

Elise watched her, assessing her as she sipped again. Her tongue captured a stray droplet of the fizzing liquid. Jasmine forced a smile; she didn't want to ruin what would be an exciting night for Elise.

'One glass won't kill you,' Elise went on. 'I'm driving, so you don't have to worry about safety.'

'I don't want one.' She couldn't keep the frost out of her voice.

Elise sighed. 'I'm not trying to push you. I'm just saying that it's OK to let your hair down every once in a while. You know—live a little. Maybe act like you're twenty-seven instead of seventy-seven.'

'I'm sure there are seventy-seven-year-olds who are more fun than me.'

Both girls laughed, and Elise hooked her arm through Jasmine's. 'Yeah, I'm going to trade you in at a nursing home on the way back.'

The room filled up around them. A woman in a knee-length indigo shift stood next to them. Jasmine was sure she'd seen her in the society pages, possibly mentioned as the wife of one of the Jaguars players. She was so close the headiness of her perfume made Jasmine breathe deep. The scent was rich. Refined. French to match the red soles of her designer shoes.

Elise nudged Jasmine and pointed out another woman

who'd walked past—a semi-celebrity, famed for the high-profile sports-star boyfriends she turned over frequently. Her tanned skin glowed as though she'd returned from the Maldives that day. She probably had.

'Why don't we sit outside? We can't take Grant's tickets and then stay in here all night.' Jasmine motioned for the door to the balcony. Her chest felt squeezed tight, as though two hands were crushing her ribcage, pushing all the air out of her. She gripped her handbag to her stomach, wishing the swishing sensation would stop.

Mercifully, Elise downed the last of her champagne and they stepped out into the members' balcony area.

The vibe outside was entirely different, and the din that rose up from the crowd was full of excitement and anticipation. Jasmine's heart immediately slowed, the pressure in her chest easing as she located two spare seats. She wrapped her coat around her shoulders and crossed her arms as she sat, popping the collar to protect her neck from the chill.

'You OK?' Elise touched her arm.

Jasmine nodded. Now that she was outside, away from the dismissive glances and claustrophobic atmosphere of the Long Room, she felt marginally better.

Still, she'd prefer to be at home with a blanket, a good book and a cup of hot chocolate. Not here, freezing her butt off in a dress that seemed to be too dressy and yet not dressy enough. But Elise could be a bulldog when she wanted to; sometimes it was easier to give in rather than indulge her Goldilocks complex about her wardrobe.

More members piled out of the Long Room and into the balcony seats. They were mostly men in suits; the women seemed to be staying inside, except for a group of younger girls with extra-long hair extensions and too-short dresses. They occupied the front row, giggling and pointing as the players took to the field.

It was match time, and the fans were chomping at the bit. The Jaguars had won the coin toss and the players now jogged into position. The noise level in the stadium swelled. Even Jasmine couldn't help but get caught up in the rush…just a little.

For some reason her stomach fluttered at the thought of seeing Grant out there. She jumped as the siren sounded and the game began. A centre bounce set the ball into play and the crowd was on the edge of their seats from the first few seconds.

'It's going to be a close game,' Elise said, her tone serious. 'The Jags lost by a point last time they played the Suns, and only by two or three points the time before that.'

'Since when are you such a football expert?'

'Since there are hot guys in tiny shorts.' She laughed.

Jasmine nodded. 'Where's Grant?'

She scanned the ground, looking for a familiar head of thick blond hair since that was about all she'd be able to see from the balcony. The players were quick, running at full speed as the ball flew from the centre towards the goalposts at one end. There was a mad scramble and the ball went out of play.

'He's the full forward.' Elise pointed to the other end of the field. 'Number eighteen.'

Jasmine spotted Grant's hulking frame, his arms bulging in the sleeveless Jaguars guernsey. His muscles rippled as he moved, tense and ready to spring into action. She noticed one of his shoulders was covered in tattoos—something she hadn't seen beneath the T-shirts he wore to her lessons. His blond hair shone under the stadium lights, and even at such a great distance she could see the focus on his face.

Her stomach clenched.

He was so masculine out there. So powerful. He moved with all the strength and grace of the big cat his team was named after. Each movement was practised and precisely executed. He tracked the other players effortlessly, moving to cover and dodge with incredible agility.

She swallowed, pushing down the attraction humming through her. He was so...*virile*.

The ball hurtled towards Grant. He sprang into action. It bounced, there was a flurry of arms and legs, and then he got his hands on it. He kicked. The ball sailed into the air, straight through the goalposts in a single graceful arc.

Around her the crowd roared; flags and scarves waved in a blur of black and green. She jumped to her feet and cheered. The air rushed out of her lungs as she shouted his name.

The players clapped one another on the back and Grant looked up towards the members' area. Jasmine was certain he was looking straight at her. OK, so maybe she *did* get the appeal of the footballer...

CHAPTER FOUR

GRANT'S MUSCLES WERE FREED, tired and a little bruised—just the way he liked it after a good massage. Most of the guys in his team booked their treatments around the schedule of a pretty brunette masseuse, but Grant much preferred the stout, middle-aged woman with knuckles of steel.

He gave his shoulders a tentative roll. They moved better than they had an hour ago, but he was tender to the touch. The game against the Suns had done a number on him. He'd pushed himself harder than ever, stretching himself beyond where he'd thought his limits were.

And all because he'd known Jasmine was watching.

Pushing thoughts of her from his mind, he walked into the reception area. People huddled at the front door, waiting for a break in the weather before they made a dash out to the car park. Rain pelted against the glass doors and lightning flashed amongst heavy clouds, illuminating the small patches of sky peeking through.

He smiled at the receptionist as she handed him a form to sign, her eyes inviting him to linger. He didn't bother. He was far too preoccupied to engage in flirtation.

His mind was on other things—namely the fact that he couldn't get a certain ballet teacher out of his head. It had been years since he'd felt genuine attraction to a woman—years since he'd had the urge to pursue a woman for something other than sex…though sex would definitely be involved.

When his ex-fiancée, Chelsea, had left him, abandoning their five-year relationship, it had felt like losing his family all over again. Since then he'd reassessed his approach to women. She'd departed with nothing but a scrawled note. He'd responded by limiting himself to a string of football groupies who were more about scratching an itch than genuine attraction. If he didn't invest in a relationship then he couldn't have it thrown back in his face. They all wanted to use him for something, so he kept them at a distance. He kept *everyone* at a distance.

Grant glanced back to the group of people waiting at the door and noticed a slender figure with a long black ponytail. *Jasmine.*

He scrawled his name on the form with haste and handed it back to the receptionist. He walked to the front of the room and slipped into the group until he stood directly behind her. She titled her head to the side and her ponytail swished against her back like a thick band of silk.

'Don't tell me you walked today.' He leant forwards, his lips all but brushing her ear. The flowery scent of her perfume immediately made his stomach flip.

She turned. Her cheeks were flushed and a black smudge ran across her upper cheek.

'I learned my lesson last time.' She managed a smile, but it didn't crinkle the corners of her eyes as it usually did. Her arms were crossed tight across her chest, though it was stuffy and warm inside the waiting room. Her mouth was a harsh line, the corners downturned slightly.

'Is everything OK?'

'I'm fine.'

Grant didn't miss the way her body stiffened next to his.

'Somehow I don't believe you.' Something within Grant

shifted as Jasmine looked at him, her face a mask of forced composure.

'Great game, by the way.' The catch in her words made him want to wrap his arms around her. He fought back the urge and shoved his hands into his pockets. 'You killed it out there.'

'The Suns didn't stand a chance.' He grinned, puffing his chest out. 'And nice attempt at changing the subject.' He nudged her in the ribcage with his elbow.

'Am I that transparent?'

'Yeah.' He reached out and ran his thumb along the black line on her cheek. 'Plus you have a little smudge on your face.'

'I'm fine.' Her eyes were wide, cheekbones flushed where he'd touched her a moment ago. Her breath hitched.

'Don't tell me you're fine when you're clearly not.'

She shook her head, looking towards the doors. He had the feeling that if he didn't grab on to her then she might bolt through the clinic's entrance into the rain. Usually it was he who had the itch to run, but not now.

He slung an arm around her shoulders as though they were old friends. The gesture should have felt platonic, safe…but the way she automatically pressed into his side felt anything but safe.

'Let me take you for a coffee. It'll make you feel better.'

Her faced tilted up to his. 'That's very sweet, but I'm OK. Honestly, I don't need your help.'

'You know you're only supposed to say "honestly" if you're telling the truth, right?'

She poked her tongue out at him.

'Just coffee, then, and I won't try to help.' He grinned. 'In fact I'll be actively unhelpful if that makes you feel better.'

'Persistent, aren't you?' She rolled her eyes at him, but she couldn't hide the smile tugging at her lips.

'Yes.'

'Is there any chance you'll take no for an answer?'

'Never.'

'I *guess* I could use the caffeine.'

He took the opportunity and linked his arm through hers. 'Let's make a break for it. We'll go in my car.'

Pushing forwards, he opened the doors against the raging wind and held Jasmine close. She shrieked as the rain hit them head-on, and they rushed down the pavement towards the car park. The ground was slippery and he held her tight so that her body bumped against him as they sprinted.

'Quickly!' she cried, her black hair whipping around her face like wet ebony ribbons.

He pulled her towards the second row of cars and fumbled with his keys. Jasmine let go of him, dashing around to the passenger side. The doors slammed loudly as they fell into the car in a rush, their breathing fogging up the windows of the Mercedes. Jasmine's laugh was a punch to his gut; even drenched and puffing she was a vision.

'Bloody Melbourne!' Grant rolled down the driver's windows and backed the car out of its spot. 'I can't see a damn thing!'

'It's freezing.' Jasmine rubbed her hands together, breathing on them. 'I swear it's going to snow this winter.'

'Fat chance.' Grant pulled the car out onto the street. 'I've never seen snow in the burbs.'

'Are you always so literal?' Her voice was teasing and Grant glanced at her sideways. A smirk passed over her face.

'Men are wired that way.' He laughed. 'Simple creatures, we are.'

'Yeah, you *are* pretty simple.'

He gave her a mock wounded expression. 'I'll have you know I'm a man of many skills.'

'Such as?'

'I solved a Rubik's cube once.'

'Really?' She raised an eyebrow at him.

'Yeah. I may have peeled off some of the colours and stuck them back down so the sides matched...'

'That's resourceful.'

'I was four.'

'I'm surprised your parents didn't get you admitted to Mensa with skills like that.'

'Who says they didn't?'

'You're a clown.' Her laughter was like bells tinkling. 'And here I was, thinking that all footballers were big oafs with more brawn than brains.'

'That's a bit judgmental.' Grant pulled the car in front of a café. 'I'm rethinking this offer.'

It was an idle threat; no way was he giving up the opportunity to get into Jasmine's head. She was too much of a puzzle for him not to have a go. He wanted to see what she was all about underneath the defensive exterior.

'Too late.' She grinned at him and leapt out of the car.

The café was one of those too-trendy-for-their-own-good places, with a coffee menu that had more options than a pizza joint had toppings. Grant normally avoided them like the plague, but he couldn't deny how amazing the coffee was. Besides, a small part of him wanted Jasmine to be impressed with his taste. Outside the studio he had the opportunity to be her equal rather than her student.

'Oh, I've been meaning to come here,' she said, shrugging off her coat and unwinding her scarf.

Grant bit back the desire to touch her as she exposed delicate ivory skin. She was utterly sensual even when doing the most mundane thing.

'It gets great reviews on a bunch of coffee blogs.'

The smooth porcelain of her neck begged to be touched, to be marked with the hunger of his kiss.

'It's good.' Grant signalled to the waiter that they wanted a table for two. 'If you can put up with the hipster vibe.'

The café was filled with people in skinny jeans and ironic T-shirts, sporting all manner of moustaches and thick-framed glasses. It certainly wasn't somewhere where he'd fit in, but he'd put up with the pretentious patrons for a decent macchiato. Plus, he was unlikely to be recognised somewhere like this—somewhere where football wasn't the religion of choice. The last thing he wanted was anyone interrupting them.

'I might not be able to read the menu.' She followed him to an empty table by the window. 'Can't say I've ever heard of *syphon* coffee before.'

'It's lighter than regular espresso 'cause the beans are roasted at a lower temperature—it's good stuff.'

'Wow.' Jasmine looked impressed. 'You should have gone with the coffee facts instead of the Rubik's cube story.'

'I stand by my choice.'

An awkward silence descended on the table. He rubbed a hand along his jaw, feeling the scratch of stubble against his palm. The café buzzed around them, full of people escaping the weather. Their table had a view of the empty rain-drenched street, and tucked away in the back he could pretend it was just the two of them.

Jasmine toyed with the single flower that sat in a jar in front of them. Her fingers brushed the blood-red blossom and the petals sprang back into position as she moved her hand away.

'Are you going to tell me what's wrong?' The words came out of Grant's mouth before he could stop them. She looked out of the window, her eyes shadowed.

'I thought you said you weren't going to help.' She

turned back to him with a small smile. 'I distinctly remember the words "actively unhelpful" being uttered.'

'I *did* say that.'

'I don't want to talk about it.' Jasmine quietened as the waiter took their orders. 'It's not something you can help with, so I don't see the point of going over it.'

'Try me.'

He couldn't tell if she was annoyed or if he was finally breaking through. Her eyebrows were knitted together and she tapped her fingernails against the edge of the table. Each nail was a glimmering pale pink. *Perfection right down to her damn fingernails.*

She was getting to him, making him want to see what secret she kept so close to her chest, what pain she hid from the world. He was drawn to her in some primal, uncontrollable way. But there was nothing he could do to sate that desire—not unless he wanted to cross a line he'd promised himself he wouldn't. Jasmine was complex. She played her cards close to her chest and she hadn't asked him for a single thing. That put her in a special category all of her own, and that meant he couldn't treat her the way he treated others.

'You *are* persistent, aren't you?' she said.

'It's one of my many qualities.'

Her dark lashes fluttered as two dots of pink formed on her cheeks. 'I am familiar with your other qualities.'

'What have you got to lose?'

Would she put up a wall between them and close him out? He wanted so desperately to delve beneath the surface, to see past the barrier she put between them. Most of all he wanted to see how far down that feminine blush of hers went. Grant fiddled with the hem of his jumper.

'Why are you so curious?'

'Why are you so guarded?'

Jasmine had to laugh. If there was one thing she could

say about Grant it was that he was like a dog with a bone. The waiter set two coffees down in front of them and she eagerly reached for hers, wrapping her hands around the warm terracotta-coloured cup.

The familiar clutches of grief tugged at her chest, closing their cold hands around her heart and lungs—making it difficult to breathe.

'Remember how I told you that I'd been in an accident?'

'Yeah.' He nodded.

'I caused it. I'd had a few drinks and argued with my boyfriend. It was stupid. I shouldn't have been driving.'

She remembered the swirl of her silk gown as she'd rushed to the car. The tears and champagne blurring her vision. The world as it tilted around her when the car rolled. The pain as she'd tried to drag herself to freedom through the driver's window.

'I don't know what to do.' Her voice was devoid of emotion. 'I can't stand the sight of alcohol anymore and I can't even take painkillers because I'm afraid to lose control.'

She held her breath, waiting to see if he would miraculously provide the solution to her problems. He didn't.

'Why do you think that taking painkillers will make you lose control?'

'You know, I'm not actually sure.' She shook her head. 'I think it started as a little game for myself when I was first recovering. I tried to wean myself off, thinking that if I could do without the painkillers then it meant I was better and I'd be able to dance again.'

'But it didn't work.' His face softened, blond lashes dropping to cover his eyes for a moment before he looked back up at her.

'No. I tried to tough it out for six months at the ballet company before I gave up. That was the worst six months of my life. I had to watch someone else dance the part I'd been given the day before the accident. It was my first lead

role—a small contemporary ballet—but it was a sign…
a sign that my career was going in the right direction. A
sign that maybe I could make it all the way to Principal.'

'Is ballet out of the question now?'

'Yeah.' She traced the opening of her coffee cup with
the pad of her finger. The smooth edges were soothing
against her skin. 'My ankle is stuffed. There was a lot of
damage to the tendons and the strength hasn't fully returned. I can't even stretch up on my toes properly, let
alone dance *en pointe*.'

'That sucks.' His hand reached over the table and clasped
hers.

The unexpected and tender gesture shocked her, while
the heat from his palm filled her body with irresistible
warmth. It spread through her, heating her chest, colour-
ing her cheeks and stirring the butterflies in her stomach.

'It's my fault.' Disappointment surged through her. 'It's
my issue to deal with—and one that I need a psychologist
for, apparently.'

For once his face showed nothing. His glacial blue eyes
were fixed on her, his blond lashes still as he looked at her
as though he were seeing past her exterior. She shifted in
her seat. She didn't want people to look at her like that…
as if they could see the darkness inside.

'Maybe seeing a psychologist wouldn't be such a bad
thing. At least he'd be trained to listen and help you work
through the problem.'

'The problem is not in my head,' she said, her teeth
grinding together. Her white-knuckled grip shook the coffee cup in her hands. 'The problem is my leg, not my brain.
I don't need to see a psychologist. This is what I've been
saying.'

She couldn't believe he was agreeing with the doctor.
Could no one see where the real issue was? She wasn't

crazy, or delusional, or incapable of understanding what had happened. The problem was in her leg. End of story.

'Has it occurred to you that perhaps you can have pain in two places at once?'

Grant leant forwards and locked his eyes on Jasmine. His raw power stopped her in the midst of her tirade. 'Life would be a lot easier if we only ever had to deal with the physical, but unfortunately it's not that simple. You need to get over those narrow-minded notions and start dealing with the problem from all angles.'

Her eyes widened at the roughness of his voice. Each word was like silk over gravel: luxurious, rugged.

'Quite the bossy-boots, aren't you?' She spoke down to her coffee cup.

The intensity in his words belied the calm mask he wore. Passion simmered in the depths of his eyes, and his hand was gripping hers like a vice. Jasmine removed her hand and sipped her drink, using the time to think up a response to Grant's argument. Well, something other than calling him a bossy-boots.

His reaction shocked her. It had been a long time since someone had told her to get over herself. In fact she couldn't remember a time where anyone in her life had said something even remotely similar to her. Even Elise had gone easy on the whole recovery subject.

They were usually too busy walking on eggshells around her to be honest. Grant spoke his mind. She liked that about him. His humorous, carefree nature was a bit of a farce. Deep down he was a fiery person, opinionated and caring. Much more than his cocky demeanour had led her to expect, and definitely more than the football stereotype would suggest.

She'd underestimated him.

Shaking her head, she looked up. His thick brows were crinkled, his eyes trained on hers. He looked so sincere she wanted to grab his face and kiss the worry away. Her lips tingled with anticipation as she fought back the urge to lean over the table and press her mouth against his. Every cell in her body craved his touch, tingling so that she couldn't ignore the effect he had on her.

Fighting back the powerful wave of attraction, she asked, 'Have you ever done something so stupid that you wished every day you could take it back?'

'Some thing*s*,' he said, stressing the *s*. 'I've made every mistake in the book.'

'Really?' She tilted her head, watching the way his large hands toyed with the small espresso cup.

For a moment she was lost in wondering what those hands would feel like on her, cradling the curve of her neck, smoothing down the length of her back, stroking her hair. Heat swelled in her, causing her to shift in her seat for a different reason this time. He was not the person she'd predicted when he'd walked into her studio that first day.

'Yeah, you take a boy out of the country and drop him smack-bang in the middle of city life and it's bound to make him go crazy. Add to that the lack of parenting, the money, the girls, the parties… Hell, I wanted to try it all at once.'

'That's understandable.'

'It's understandable to want to *try* it all.' He offered up a rueful smile. 'It's another thing to actually do it.'

'Isn't it just part of being a footballer?' she asked. 'Aren't you all known for your antics?'

'I'd rather be known for playing good footy.'

'I'm pretty sure you're known for that already.' She wanted to comfort him, the same way he had done for her, but she didn't know where to start. Her hand fluttered in her lap.

'It wouldn't be so bad if it weren't so damn public. Everyone makes mistakes, but ours are documented by the media. And once it's out there you can't ever erase it.'

His face darkened when he mentioned the media, and for the first time Jasmine felt as if she might be on exactly the same plane as Grant. Her family and friends had brought her magazines and newspapers to keep her busy while she was in hospital, and one day she'd seen a picture of her ex with a new woman on his arm. Another ballerina—a girl she'd known since she was a child. It wasn't the media's fault, sure, but if they didn't report on every single little happening in people's lives she might have been spared that gut-wrenching pain for a while longer.

'So tell me about football,' she said, eager to change the topic and see Grant's face return to its normal unstressed state. 'Do you think you'll make finals this year?'

'That's certainly the plan. Some guys don't like to call it early, in case they jinx it, but I don't think it's possible to get out of bed and train as hard as we do if you don't believe you can get there.'

Oh, how she envied his confidence. She'd been like that once.

'I'm sure it's the same with dancing. The physical aspect is only one part. These things are as much about the mental game as they are about the training and the practice.'

'Looks like we're not so different after all.' She smiled, trying to keep the tone light, but it struck her how similar their lives were once you got past the superficial differences.

He drained the last of his coffee and set the cup down on the table, the smile back on his face. 'Another?'

'I should probably get you to take me back to my car.' She shook her head. 'I appreciate your honesty, by the way—a lot of people are too busy pitying me to give me a kick up the butt when I need it.'

She detected a hint of uncertainty as he smiled back at

her—there was definitely something going on behind those glacial blue eyes of his—but he managed to keep himself behind a wall even while he coaxed her to let her own guard down. She wanted to know more, but it had been so long since she'd had a man in her life who wanted anything from her aside from the physical that she wasn't quite sure how to ask the questions that swirled inside her head.

'My pleasure.' He stood and manoeuvred his hulking frame between the crammed tables of the café. 'Butt-kicking is a speciality of mine.'

'Cheating a Rubik's cube, random coffee facts and butt-kicking…it's an unusual skill set, I'll give you that.'

As they made their way to the counter to pay for their coffees an icy breeze blew in from the street. The rain had calmed, but the temperature was still low enough to slice straight to the bone. She huddled instinctively against Grant, seeking out warmth and protection. He wrapped an arm around her shoulders and pulled her closer while he fixed up the bill. She felt good nestled against him—as if nothing could get to her. The unexpected familiarity of his embrace made her mouth run dry.

'Time to brave the cold.'

He moved his hand down to her lower back and pressed gently as they walked out into the street. They hurried to the car, their faces bowed against the wind, and Jasmine stayed close to Grant right until they reached the passenger door.

Once inside the car she was acutely aware of their proximity, of the way his jeans hugged his strong thighs and stretched across his hips. The car was hot as a sauna.

Heat pulsed between her legs as her mind gave way to the salacious fantasy of him taking her in the back seat of the Mercedes. It had occupied her ever since he'd first given her a lift.

Seemingly unaware of her erotic thoughts, Grant navigated the car onto the main road and headed in the direction of the doctor's clinic. She allowed her eyes to slip downwards, over his broad chest and down...

'See something you like down there?'

His voice caused Jasmine to snap her head back up to the windscreen. Her cheeks flamed as she realised she'd been caught in the act. *Jasmine Bell, your mother would be ashamed!*

His gravelly laugh set fire to her belly, the embarrassment and desire mingling into one confused knot of emotion. He was cocky—but with that kind of intense sexual power she couldn't blame him. Her eyes flickered up to his face. His lips were parted with hunger but his eyes were focused on the road ahead, although he glanced at her whenever they stopped at a red light.

She'd seen something else today: the tenderness in the way he'd covered her hand with his. He'd cared for her, even if only for a split second. Like the bump in his nose, there was a crack in the image he presented—a softness beneath the tough outer shell and she'd glimpsed it today. Part of her wanted to reach in and pull him apart, to see what he was made of. The other part of her knew what his life would be like—glamour, paparazzi, wealth. And she couldn't go there...not again.

CHAPTER FIVE

JASMINE THREW HERSELF into the choreography for the EJ Ballet School's annual Winter Performance. It was something to focus her energy on—something other than fighting off the pulse-racing thoughts of Grant interrupting her day. She needed a project, a reason to wake up in the morning, something to pour her heart and soul into.

The routine was coming together well, and she'd finished her first lesson with the four teachers who would be performing it.

'How come you're not dancing with us?' one of the teachers asked, snapping Jasmine's attention back to the present.

'Jasmine has an injury,' Elise said, steering the teacher towards the exit of the studio. 'I made her promise that she'd get better before she put any pressure on herself to perform.'

Details of her accident had been kept quiet when Elise had brought her onto the teaching staff. Not because she necessarily had anything to hide but because she was still recovering emotionally and physically. Not much had changed in six months.

The teachers gave Jasmine a wave as they left the studio. She followed them out to the waiting room so she could relax before Grant arrived. Dropping down to one knee, she sighed as she rifled through her sports bag. Her fingertips brushed the roughened satin of her *pointe* shoes and she pulled one out. They were the shoes from her first professional performance as a member of the *corps de ballet* all those years ago. The satin had split and frayed around the shoe's box, and the shank was broken, but she hadn't been able to throw them away. Elise had signed the soles in her flowery cursive, and Jasmine had done the same to Elise's first shoes.

It was days like this that made her wonder if she should give it up all together. She loved choreography but the wounds were still wide open. It hurt so damn much not to join in as the teachers danced her steps. Once again she was sitting on the sidelines, wasting all the sacrifices her parents had made to help her get where she was.

A sudden impulse made her put the shoes on; she lovingly tied the ribbons around her ankle and stood. They felt comfortable, and since she wouldn't be able to rise up *en pointe* anyway the broken shank didn't matter. She twirled on the spot, practising the steps from her new routine. Her body warmed and the glow she always felt when she danced spread through her. The world seemed more beautiful when she danced; her troubles evaporated and she was at peace.

'That's pretty damn good.'

Grant's voice came from behind her. She'd been so lost in the movement she hadn't even heard him come in. 'I bet you say that to all the girls.'

'I don't have to say anything.' He grinned that delicious crooked grin of his. 'The girls usually drop to my feet as I walk past.'

Jasmine rolled her eyes. It bothered her that despite his sarcasm it was probably the truth. And why *wouldn't* girls drop at his feet? Football players were practically the *crème de la crème* of Australian society. Many women craved the spotlight and the access dating a footballer would provide…but not her. For a moment she wished he was an ordinary guy, rather than a famous athlete. Why couldn't he be someone who could walk down the street unnoticed?

'You'd better be careful—if your head gets much bigger you won't be able to get out of the building.' She dropped to the ground and removed the *pointe* shoes, slipping her feet back into her soft split-soles.

'These are like proper ballet shoes, aren't they?' Grant picked up one of the *pointe* shoes and examined it as though it were a piece of an alien spacecraft. 'The real deal.'

Jasmine nodded. 'They are the real deal indeed.'

'You miss it a lot, don't you?' He turned the shoe in his hand, touching it as though it were the most precious thing in the world.

Her stomach flipped. 'Yeah, I do.'

'And you can't go back?'

The studio hummed in the midst of their silence, a broken light flickering overhead. She held out her hand and he handed over the shoe. The familiar shape of it in her palm caused her breath to hitch. She packed it away safely in her bag and forced a smile.

'You didn't come here to talk about this.' She motioned for him to follow her into the studio. 'Let's get to work.'

He opened his mouth but then closed it again, a curious expression on his face. She gave herself a little shake to bring her back to the present. She didn't want his pity, and he wasn't here to listen to her sob story. Again.

'Today I'm going to teach you a new step,' she said, focusing her attention on business. 'The *relevé* is a position with the feet together at the ankles, heels lifted from the ground.'

Jasmine rose up onto her toes, her ankles crossed. She wasn't able to rise as high as she'd used to, but it was enough to show the intention of the step. Her ankle groaned under the position, warning her not to push too far.

He followed along, but wobbled before he could fully stretch up. She stepped closer and put her hand on the flat of his stomach.

'You have to activate your core muscles,' she said. His abs flexed under her touch as he stabilised himself, sending a frisson of excitement racing through her. 'You're strong here. You need to keep your body centred otherwise you won't be able to balance.'

He smirked and heat flooded her cheeks. It was impossible for her to forget what he looked like on the field, his body primed and masculine. Her every nerve-ending fired with need, betraying the sensible restrictions her mind enforced.

'Try again,' she said, doing her best to sound professional.

But she couldn't draw her hand from his stomach. It was stuck there, as though forced by some invisible magnetic energy.

As Grant worked to keep himself stable he rose taller and stretched so that he could look clean over the top of her head.

'Much better.'

'Show me one more time?'

Grant's eyes were locked on her; her skin tingled everywhere they travelled.

'Of course.' Jasmine pulled her shoulders back and relaxed her body into a perfect turn-out. Bending down, she extended her knees outwards and brought her feet into *relevé,* her ankles crossed as she balanced without a tremor of unsteadiness.

Grant stepped forwards, his hand reaching out to touch her stomach in the same way she had touched his. His full lips parted as he stepped close to her. 'Yes, very stable.'

They stood frozen—neither bold enough to make the next move. Jasmine held her breath. She didn't want to move in case he might withdraw his hand and break the spell, yet she trembled at the thought of what she would do if he didn't pull back.

Grant moved his hand down to her waist, tilting his

body into hers so that their faces were only inches apart. She could smell the spice of his aftershave and the subtle mint on his breath. She could easily give in, draw her hand up to his chest and submit.

There was something utterly disarming about him. The combination of his strong jaw and the slightly crooked, freckle-smattered nose enchanted her. He was real and unabashedly male, unlike many of the effeminate boys she'd grown up with.

'Are you ready to do it on your own?' Jasmine dropped down from the position so she was an inch or two below eye level with Grant. She tried to unscramble her senses, to focus on the lesson.

'I can.' His voice was low, predatory. 'But don't you think it's much more fun when we do it together?'

The air between them was thick with electricity, its gravitational pull unravelling her sensibilities. She so desperately wanted to touch him. Her mouth was dry, anticipation making her pulse race.

He placed his hands over hers and Jasmine jumped at the way her blood pulsed harder and harder.

'Why so jumpy? Are you uncomfortable being alone with me?'

'No,' she whispered.

The problem was she was far too comfortable as he stood close to her. All she wanted to do was melt against him. She envisaged herself pressing against his broad chest and sturdy thighs. Her entire body crackled with excitement as they stood, merely inches apart, in the empty ballet studio.

Why was she feeling like this? He was out of her league—in a league she never wanted to be a part of again. Ever, *ever* again.

He reached his hands up to her face, cupping the sides of her cheeks in his palms. It was the wrong thing to do;

she shouldn't be going down this path. But desire raced through her veins and filled her with irresistible warmth, overpowering logic. He was intoxicating.

Up close, she felt the pull of his hypnotic stare. The endless blue of his eyes made the rest of the world fall away. It made sense and reason evaporate. Her lips parted.

Grant drew Jasmine's face to his in a swift and practised movement. Her eyes fluttered closed as his mouth came down. The soft fullness of his lips pressed hungrily against hers, his tongue hot and probing. Jasmine sighed into him. It had been so long since she'd been kissed, and a lifetime since she'd been kissed in a way that made her weak in the knees.

Grant moved one hand from her face, down the length of her arm, and snaked it around her waist, drawing her closer to him. Every inch of her burned as their bodies fused together, the thinness of their workout clothes mimicking the deliciousness of skin on skin. Her hands found their way into the wavy depths of his golden-blond hair. It was thick and silken against her palms. Her fingers gripped tightly as he dipped her, demanding deeper access to her mouth.

His breath was hot on her face as his lips moved down her jawline to the slender column of her neck, each kiss searing her skin. He backed her up until she pressed against the wall of the studio, crushed between plaster and the hardness of him.

He worked back to her mouth, tugging at her lower lip and flicking his tongue against hers. He tasted of mint, smelled of spices and earthy maleness. Blood coursed through her, hot and thick, as he devoured her. His hand skimmed her hips, reaching around to curve against her ass. He pressed her to him, the thick length of his arousal digging into her belly. She moved her hips against him, dragging a guttural plea from his lips.

'You taste so good,' he murmured against her mouth, drawing out the syllables of the last word. '*Feel* so good.'

Her tongue traced the sharp angle of his jaw. The golden hairs of his stubble were rough against her. She wanted to lick every inch of him…every single inch. She clamped her eyes shut and lost herself.

His thigh nudged her legs open and she gasped. His hand smoothed up the side of her, traversing over her ribcage and palming her breast. Her nipples pebbled in response, desperate for skin-to-skin contact. His thumb brushed the hardened peak, pushing her further into oblivion. This was the most pleasure she had allowed herself since the accident.

Visions of them flooded her…their bodies slick with sweat, limbs entwined. Panting. Writhing. Aching. She'd never wanted something with such desperation in all her life.

She could envisage how breathtaking he would be when he was naked, but it was the image of herself naked that jolted her out of her reverie.

Her leg.

Picturing the mangled piece of flesh she called her right leg halted her thoughts. The long snakelike red scar would stand out angrily against her paleness. The skin itself was ruined, never again to be smooth and supple like the rest of her. There was no way he'd find her attractive after that—how could he?

She looked like a freak show.

Pressure mounted in her chest as she brought her two palms flat against his chest and pushed hard. Grant stumbled backwards, a look of utter shock and surprise on his face—his blue eyes swam with confusion.

'I'm—I'm sorry,' she stammered. 'I can't—'

Pushing past him, Jasmine sprinted from the room, only stopping to scoop up her bag as she bolted for the exit.

* * *

'I ran out of there like an idiot.' Jasmine shook her head as she raised a jumbo coffee cup to her lips. 'Tragic.'

Elise stared at Jasmine—wide-eyed and open-mouthed—while her coffee sat on the table, untouched. Her grey eyes were unblinking as she processed this new information. 'Let me get this straight. The Football Hunk had you pinned up against a wall and you bailed? What's wrong with you?'

The café around them buzzed with activity. They'd managed to get a table that was off to one side, giving them a semblance of privacy, though Jasmine still lowered her voice.

'I think I'm broken.' She nursed the steaming coffee in both hands.

Elise patted her arm across the small round table. 'You're not broken.'

Elise had called at her house at the crack of dawn because she'd found Jasmine's mobile phone and boots in the studio. Elise's conclusion upon finding the items—perhaps not logical, though not unusual for Elise—was that Jasmine had been kidnapped. So her tale of failed seduction was a welcome alternative.

'You know what freaked me out the most?' Jasmine said as she traced her finger around the rim of her coffee cup, forehead creased. 'All I could think about was my leg. What would happen if he saw it? How would he react?'

Her voice wavered. For so long her body had been a source of success and pleasure—she'd *never* despised the way she looked. Sure, she'd wished at times that her boobs had developed past an A cup, but a flat chest was something that went with being a ballerina. She'd never felt the crippling wash of shame that she had last night. Jasmine put her cup down and dropped her chin into her hands.

'At some point you're going to have to get past that...

unless you plan on being a spinster and filling your house with stray cats, of course.'

A smile twitched on Jasmine's lips. The one thing she loved about Elise was her strength of character. She looked soft and sweet as a marshmallow, but there was an iron will packed into that petite package. She was often the only one who could give Jasmine the straight-up truth. Her parents, her friends at the ballet company and even her teachers had sugar-coated the news from the doctors. They'd instilled a false sense of hope while she recovered. It had been born out of love, sure, but sometimes she needed the cold, hard truth delivered with an empathetic smile and a pat on the back.

'I know.' Jasmine brought the cup to her lips, inhaling the comforting coffee scent before taking a sip. 'I get that I have to move past it. But how can I expect any man to look past it when I can't even do that myself?'

'That's my point exactly.' Elise grabbed her hand, wrapping her slender fingers around Jasmine's palm and squeezing. 'Maybe what you need is to realise the world won't implode if you get naked. It's not going to get all apocalyptic if someone sees your leg. Perhaps getting this guy into bed is exactly what you need to move on? If you can see that it's not a big deal to the other person then maybe it won't be such a big deal to you.'

'Sex as therapy?' Jasmine tilted her head. 'Is that a thing?'

'No idea.' Elise took a big gulp from her latte. 'What's the worst it can do? You have a little no-strings fun, enjoy yourself, and if you're still having issues over the leg thing then maybe we need to get you some professional help.'

'I am *not* seeing a shrink.' Jasmine glared. Elise was pushing her buttons on purpose.

Going to a psychologist would be like admitting that she'd fallen apart and didn't have the ability to fix the problem herself. It was the ultimate sign of weakness. No, there was no way she was doing that. Sex as therapy seemed like a much more enjoyable way to deal with it—not to mention it wouldn't send her broke.

'What have you got to lose?'

'My dignity?' Jasmine shook her head.

There was no way she could proposition Grant. What if he laughed at her?

'Did he initiate the kiss last night?'

'Well, yes, but—'

'No buts.' Elise slapped her palm down on the table and the coffee cups clattered against their saucers. 'Do you want to be a crazy cat lady?'

People at the nearby tables looked over, not even bothering to hide their curiosity. Jasmine let out a laugh.

'I'll think about it.'

'How long has it been, anyway?'

Only Elise would ask such a personal question in the middle of a café.

'Too long.' *Too damn long.*

The idea of propositioning Grant was making her sweat. It was well outside the realm of her fairly limited experience. She hadn't had sex since she'd broken off her relationship with Kyle Waterhouse, and before him there had only been one other awkward experience with a boy she'd had a crush on at school.

Sex had certainly taken a back seat while she was dancing. Her focus had always been; ballet first, boys second. Her nickname 'Queen Bun-Head' had been well earned.

Needless to say she'd never openly propositioned anyone before…let alone for a one-night stand with a psychological agenda.

Elise seemed satisfied that Jasmine was at least willing to give her plan some thought, though Jasmine had no idea how she would approach Grant. Would he even want to be around her after she'd run off like a crazy person last night?

Probably not.

Fear, excitement and doubt knotted in her stomach, each emotion fighting to overtake the others. Jasmine tapped her nails against the hard wood of the café table while she played the situation out in her head.

'Don't be nervous,' Elise said, waving her hand dismissively. 'If he tries to say no—and I highly doubt he will—remind him how flexible ballerinas are. That should do the trick!'

'You might be on to something there.' Jasmine laughed. 'But I haven't committed to anything, remember?'

'Sure, sure.' Elise waved her hand as if to dismiss Jasmine's comment. She picked up her cup and drained the last of her coffee. 'I need to head off.' Elise stood, bundling up her trench coat and handbag. 'I've got a date with the costume designer to talk through the final alterations for our swans.'

'Have fun with that.' Jasmine finished her coffee and joined Elise.

'You'd better give me an update on Operation Hunky Footballer Seduction,' Elise said as they left the bustling café, squeezing their way through the crowd and onto the street. 'I want details!'

'Is that what we're calling it now?'

'Has a good ring to it, I think.' Elise giggled and waved as she headed off in the opposite direction to Jasmine.

'I said I'd think about it,' Jasmine called after her as she headed off towards the car, with excitement putting a spring in her step.

CHAPTER SIX

GRANT SAT IN his car, his body defiantly rooted to the driver's seat of the Mercedes. Since his close encounter with Jasmine he'd been unable to think of anything else. Her glossy black hair and those enormous sparkly brown eyes filled his every waking moment.

Never before had a woman left him high and dry like that. Hell, one of the main perks of being a football player was that the girls lined up for him. But Jasmine Bell was a lady unlike any of the women he usually fell into bed with. She was a breath of fresh air and a thorn in his side. She'd responded to his advances with surprising gusto and then she'd run without explanation.

What the hell?

Drumming his fingers on the dash, Grant let out a long breath and forced himself out of the driver's seat and towards the studio. Inside it was quiet. Elise was chatting to a student and acknowledged him with a smile as he dropped his bag onto the waiting room couch. Jasmine was in the studio, stepping out the choreography he'd seen her practising the other night.

If she hadn't told him about her injury he would never have known from watching her. She seemed perfectly steady on her feet as she danced. It was like peering into a very private part of her world—in some ways like watching her undress. It couldn't have been further from his initial impression that ballet was stilted and boring. She moved with an effortless grace, swanlike in her fluid yet precise movement.

Each move was filled with raw passion and sensuality. He couldn't have looked away even if his life had depended on it. It was a crime that she couldn't perform; he could only imagine how incredible she would have looked on a stage. Was there nothing she could do? He wondered what he would have done if his mistakes had ruined his career instead of just his reputation.

She paused to study the piece of paper in one hand. Concentration narrowed her eyes, and her focus was reflected in the wall-to-wall mirror. As she worked through a problem she melted into the movement.

Remember the rule: no attachment. They all want something.

It was true; all the people he allowed into his life were after something. Distant acquaintances wanted members' tickets, the women he bedded wanted access to VIP lounges, old friends wanted money for a snippet of his history and Chelsea... All she'd wanted was a stepping stone to the next big thing. Even his best friend had sold out for a chance at the spotlight, flipping on him and leaving him alone at the worst possible moment. Funny that when he needed their help these people were nowhere to be found.

Grant closed his eyes to shut out the painful memories. Tempting as Jasmine was, history had taught him that commitment was dangerous, and something deep down told him that one taste of Jasmine wouldn't be enough. That was if his reactions to date were anything to go on.

The kiss had been a slip-up, confirming that she was definitely in the look-but-don't-touch-because-its-too-damn-tempting basket. He couldn't afford to let anything take his mind off football—not when his career and reputation were hanging in the balance.

Even now, as he steeled himself with resolve, the thought of having her for even one night filled him with an indescribable heat. A silent, familiar voice urged him on—just one taste.

He hadn't experienced urges like that in quite a while—the urges to consume, to lose himself in pleasure, to blank out the loneliness.

He shook his head. He couldn't give in because it was that same voice that told him it was OK to have another drink, another night on the town, another nameless woman in his bed. He couldn't trust that voice.

Jasmine held herself straight, struggling to keep her breathing steady. With each lesson it was becoming harder to maintain control, to preserve the distance between her and Grant. Elise's suggestion weighed down on her, luring her with the possibility of revisiting that intoxicating kiss. The memory of his palms pressing her against the studio wall sent delicious shivers down her spine.

Now, as he watched her through the window, she couldn't help the spiral of delight that shot through her. Her body tingled when he entered the studio, crossing the large space in a handful of long-legged strides, his broad shoulders a magnet for her attention. She was pretty sure it should be illegal to be that good-looking.

'Ready to get those muscles moving?' she chirped, surprised when he didn't return her smile.

'I'm ready to get on with it.' His tone was dry. Different.

She wrinkled her brow and tilted her head to one side. Something was amiss. His frosty eyes were calm. Like a perfectly still lake, they reflected the outside in order to mask what lay beneath.

'Right.' She turned and walked to the *barre*, frowning. What had turned him from the man who'd pinned her up against a wall to this impersonal lump? Or perhaps that was it? He'd taken her running as a sign to stay the hell away, that she wasn't woman enough to handle one steamy kiss.

Jasmine drew a deep breath and shook her head to dislodge the negative thoughts. She was being paranoid. But a cold lump of steel wedged in her belly anyway.

As the lesson progressed he remained withdrawn, avoiding eye contact and providing single-word responses to her questions. She searched his face for a hint of warmth, but he was as cold as the winter outside.

Soon it was time to cool down and work on Grant's flexibility problems.

They sat in the middle of the floor, stretching out their hamstrings while facing one another. A flicker of pain crossed his face as he leant forwards, trying to elongate his injured muscle. He usually appeared tense when they stretched, which was strange since most people looked relieved after a ballet class. Stretching was supposed to be the enjoyable bit, but his brows were knitted together and he often gritted his teeth. Perhaps his injury was more painful than he let on?

'Is something wrong?' she asked.

He didn't make eye contact, instead focusing on the ground ahead of him. 'No.'

'You've barely said two words to me all evening.'

For someone who had been so persistent in getting her to talk, he sure was giving her the silent treatment.

'Nothing's wrong.'

Grant rolled onto his back, lifting his injured leg in the air and reaching up towards his foot. The muscle was so resistant he couldn't even get into the proper position. Without asking if he wanted help, Jasmine knelt between his legs to administer an assisted stretch. His calf rested against her shoulder and she pressed forwards slowly, feeling his hamstring muscle release.

'Is it about the kiss?'

His eyes were still frosted over. They were like two chips of ice: cold, hard-edged and unyielding. 'I'd prefer if we didn't talk about that while you're practically on top of me.'

'Don't be such a baby. I'm only helping you stretch.' She tried to ignore the fact that a few items of flimsy clothing were all that prevented them from being a *Karma Sutra* illustration.

'The kiss was a mistake.'

Jasmine swallowed, sitting back and motioning him to switch legs. 'Why?'

'Because I…I shouldn't have done it.'

'That's not an answer.' She pressed into the stretch, one hand braced on the ground next to his arm, the other holding his active leg. 'Besides, it takes two to tango.'

'If we must talk, can't it be about something else?'

'Such as?' She peered down at him while she pushed on his leg.

'How about your dancing?' He sighed, closing his eyes for a moment as Jasmine pressed slowly.

'What about it?' She leant back and motioned for him to switch legs again.

'Why are you teaching here? It's clear you've got too much talent to be teaching toddlers.'

'Why do you care?' She didn't want to get into it; her pain was not his concern.

He didn't answer. Instead, he stared at her wordlessly until she felt as if she might burn up on the spot.

'You don't want to talk about a simple kiss, but you're quite happy to talk about my personal trauma?'

He paused. 'I think you should give dancing another shot.'

'It's not that easy.' She sighed. Why did everyone think

it was as simple as that? If it were, wouldn't she have gone back by now?

'I know you can do it.'

'I want to talk about the kiss instead.' She pursed her lips.

'Why? You were the one who ran off like...like...' He grappled for words. 'I can't talk about this while you're... there.'

'This is a perfectly legitimate cool-down activity.' Maybe if she said it enough times she'd convince herself it was all for his benefit...and not because she felt compelled to be close to him.

'I should have stopped it.'

'It's not a big deal.'

'Yes, it is. I'm not looking for a relationship and I don't have the time nor the interest to have anyone in my life.' His voice was low, guarded. He was censoring himself, barricading his true feelings behind the commanding tone and blank stare. 'It was a momentary lapse of judgement.'

Jasmine sat back, startled by the complete one-hundred-and-eighty-degree turn that had taken place. It was as if she was speaking to a different person.

'I'm not looking for a relationship either.' *Hell, that's the last thing I need.*

'Trust me,' he said, standing up and dusting off his tights. His eyes raked over her, calculating and cold as he observed her reaction. 'It's for your own good.'

Heat spread from Jasmine's neck to her face. She was sure her cheeks burned red as tomatoes.

It's for your own good.

She'd heard that phrase many times in her failed relationship with Kyle Waterhouse. Her ex had been the possessive type, controlling. That had been his catchphrase. The one he'd tried on every time she rebelled against his commands. When she hadn't been allowed to wear a short dress it had been for her own good. When he'd prevented her from going out with her friends it had been for her own good. When he'd embarrassed her in front of his family by telling her she shouldn't be eating anything fattening it had been for her own good.

The statement hung thick and heavy over them, sucking the air from her lungs. She was about to lose it—about to let go of the rage that was a tight, flaming knot in her stomach.

She lowered Grant's leg to the floor and rocked back onto her heels. She rose slowly.

'What is "for my own good" is none of your concern. I take care of myself. So do us both a favour and don't tell me what to do.'

Mustering her composure, she turned and walked to the door. Heart pounding, she grabbed her coat and bag and headed out of the building. It was incredible how four little words could fill her with a boiling pot of blinding, white-hot emotion.

Wincing as the night air slapped her in the face, she tried to feel satisfaction as the door slammed shut behind her, the bang resonating out into the empty parking lot. Logically she knew that he couldn't understand the effect those words had on her, but hearing them made her want to run. Made her want to put as much distance between them as possible.

Lungs burning, she continued at pace towards Elise's car. She fumbled in her bag, hands shaking as she looked frantically for the keys—praying that he wouldn't come after her.

She'd deluded herself, tricked herself into reading something into his kiss…into the way he'd touched her hand in the café. Her insides tumbled as she realised what a fool she must look, expecting something from him that she shouldn't. Lusting after him like some starstruck teen.

Idiot, idiot, idiot!

How could she have been so naive? Was she so desperate after Kyle that she thought the next guy to kiss her was something special? Elise was right—crazy cat lady status was cemented in her future.

Heat burned her cheeks. Her vision was blurred by the puffs of white smoke that billowed up as her hot breath connected with the chilly night air. Mercifully she located the car keys and hit the unlock button. Sliding inside the car, she turned the engine over and pressed her foot to the ground. The car's tyres screeched as she raced from the car park.

He was just like the rest of them.

The EJ Ballet School's big day had arrived. Its annual Winter Performance was a matinee showcase of all the routines due to appear in the upcoming competition season. It would be Jasmine's first time back in a theatre since she left the Australian Ballet.

Her footsteps echoed, and even though she was indoors condensation billowed from her mouth as she hurried down the aisle to the first row of seats. The theatre's heating system had just kicked in, and it would take a while for the chill to wear off. Memories flooded her, and the old thrill of adrenaline that came before a performance lit up her senses.

She could see the back of Elise's head, her flaxen hair already slicked into a bun and affixed with a glittering headpiece.

Jasmine slumped down next to her. Shivering, she brought a takeaway cup to her lips. The coffee inside was strong and piping hot, exactly the way she liked it.

'Morning.' Elise was sewing a string of sequins around the hem of a costume, her golden brows knitted together while her tongue stuck out from the side of her lips.

The past few days had been like wading through sludge and the way things had been left with Grant weighed on Jasmine. She shouldn't care. It had only been a kiss. But as far as kisses went…it had been the motherload.

'Do you want to talk about it?' Elise said without looking up.

'Talk about what?'

'Why you've been moping around like a kid who's lost her puppy.' Elise continued to focus on her costume, pushing the needle through the fabric and pulling it out the other side. She threaded a sequin, then a bead, and drove the needle back down.

'I have not.'

'Don't lie to me, Jazz.' Elise paused to give her friend a withering stare. 'I can't take your denial before breakfast.'

Jasmine presented the coffee and bagel she'd picked up for Elise on her way in and let out a chuckle at the look of complete adoration that washed over her friend's face. 'No, I don't want to talk about it.'

'I think you *should* talk about it.' Elise looked up after taking a long swig of her coffee. 'Did you pitch the sex as therapy idea?'

'I didn't even get that far,' Jasmine replied, frowning.

'How come?'

'Because he back-pedalled on the whole thing. Apparently the kiss was a mistake.'

'He said that?'

'Verbatim.' Jasmine rolled her eyes. 'Then he told me he was protecting me—that he was backing off for my own good.'

Elise winced. 'I can imagine how *that* went down.'

'It was just a kiss…we're both adults…I don't see why he's got his knickers in a knot about it.'

'You were the one who bailed after you kissed.' Trust

Elise to flip it on her. 'Do you think he freaked out because of that?'

'No idea. He's hot one minute…hotter than hot…and then freezing cold the next.' Jasmine sipped on her coffee. 'I can't keep my head straight, watching him bounce back and forth.'

Both girls paused when the sound of the theatre door opening caught their attention. Missy, a long-time friend and fellow dance teacher, made her way to the girls at the front. Her skin held a sickly green tinge.

'What the hell is wrong with you?' Elise asked.

'Stomach bug,' Missy replied, and her bleary eyes showed how many times she'd got up in the middle of the night. 'I'm OK. I just need a minute—'

Her eyes bulged and she shot up from her seat, racing towards the front exit where the toilets were. Elise and Jasmine looked at one another.

'Crap.' Elise dropped her head into her hands. 'There's no way she's going to be able to pirouette without barfing on the stage. What a disaster!'

Missy was one of the quartet dancing in the teachers' routine Jasmine had choreographed. They'd been working towards this performance for weeks, and with several of the scouts from the Australian Ballet School attending everything needed to run like clockwork.

They waited until Missy returned. She curled up into a ball next to Jasmine, her teeth chattering, her skin glowing with a clammy sheen.

'We can do the dance with three people instead of four. I'll re-choreograph the partnering in the middle.'

'I'm fine,' Missy protested weakly.

Students filed into the theatre, excited voices chattering, oblivious to the problems their teachers were dealing with.

'We can't change the choreography now.' Elise shook

her head, ignoring Missy's feeble protest. 'That's way too much pressure.'

'But no one else knows the steps.'

Jasmine massaged her temples. She knew exactly what was coming.

'You do.'

The statement hung in the air, eclipsed by the sound of blood rushing in Jasmine's ears. There was no way she could step in now. She hadn't been on stage in so long and she wasn't ready for her first time to be in front of an entire ballet school's worth of family and friends.

No. No way in hell.

'I can't do it.'

'I'm sorry, Jazz.' Missy shot up from her seat again and raced through the exit.

'Yes, you *can,*' Elise implored her. 'I know you can.'

'I'm not a dancer anymore.' Jasmine's voice broke as the pressure overwhelmed her.

She jumped up and walked out of the theatre, through the foyer and into the chilly morning air. The sky was grey, storm clouds looming like a prediction of the future. Her stomach churned with guilt. She was letting Elise and the others down. But she couldn't get back out there. Not yet. Not now. No amount of puppy-dog eyes from Elise would make her do it. What if she fell? What if she'd lost all of her talent and she looked like a fool beside Elise and the other teachers? She couldn't risk that.

Damn it!

Elise had worked so hard at pulling the Winter Performance together and this wasn't fair. She deserved a better friend than Jasmine—someone who could get past her own problems and step up. But she couldn't do it. She was too broken.

'What are you going to do?'

The voice startled Jasmine and she spun around. *Grant.*

'What are you doing here?' she asked.

He was perched on the handrail that led from the theatre door to the valet area. Thigh-hugging jeans and a leather jacket that looked soft as butter clung to his frame in all the right places. His jaw was freshly shaven and his thick blond hair was mussed into a peak.

He looked hot as sin.

'I bought a ticket.' He shrugged. 'You know…supporting the community and all that.'

Jasmine couldn't stop the corners of her mouth twitching into a smile. 'Very big of you.'

'So what are you going to do?' He cocked his head to one side, waiting for her answer.

'About what?'

'If I read the situation correctly your routine is one dancer short.' He paused. 'I saw her coming out of the ladies' room…I don't think I've ever seen a person who was literally green before.'

Jasmine let out a rush of air. They were screwed. 'I don't know what we're going to do, but it's not something you need to worry about. The show must go on, as they say.'

'So you're not going to step up?'

His question sucked the breath from her. It was one thing to hear it from Elise, but it was another thing entirely for Grant to get involved. Especially since he'd made it clear the little intimacy they'd shared was something he didn't wish to repeat.

'It's not a matter of stepping up.' Jasmine folded her arms across her chest. 'I'm not a dancer anymore.'

'Yes, you are. I've seen you in that studio.'

'You don't know what it's like, Grant.'

'You crave it. You feel incomplete without it.' He stood and stepped towards her. 'Does that sound about right?'

She bit down on her lip. OK, so maybe he *did* know what she was feeling. That didn't change the situation.

'Don't you think I would have done it by now if it were that easy?' She tightened her arms, partly to warm her and partly to quell the tiny flicker of hope in her chest.

She wasn't ready. Her body wasn't ready, nor her mind... Hell, she didn't even have her ballet shoes with her.

'Nothing worth having is easy.'

'What motivation poster did you steal *that* from?' Sarcasm dripped from her voice. It was a natural defence, and right now pushing him away was easier than dealing with any of it.

She couldn't take him and his confusing hot/cold actions. She couldn't take this pressure, the competing desire and fear that somersaulted in her stomach. It was too much, too soon.

He caught her shoulders between his hands. His jaw was clenched, his eyes burning into hers. 'If you don't do it now you might not ever have the guts to perform again.'

'You don't know that.' She looked away. The cold was seeping through her clothes and into her bones. 'Why do you even care?'

'Because I've been there. I've stood on that edge, wondering whether to play it safe or take the plunge.'

'And?' She held her breath, frozen by the intensity that radiated from him and rooted her to the ground.

'It's worth it. It's worth the fear and the sacrifices you've already made to be who you need to be. You need to try again.'

Were they still talking about her dancing? Memories swirled up and shimmered before her. She'd been happy once...before she'd gambled everything on a career that had crashed and burned. What did she have to show for those years of hard work?

'I can't.'

'I thought about giving up football, you know.' He scuffed the ground with the edge of one heavy black boot.

'I dragged my team's name through the mud when I went off the rails. I remember going to training the morning after a huge blow-up and hovering at the entrance to the ground. I wasn't sure I could face them all. I wasn't sure I could risk them rejecting me.'

'This is different.' She tried to keep the surge of empathy out of her voice—this wasn't the same situation. 'I'm not hesitating because I'm worried I can't do it. I *know* I can't.'

'Yes,' he said roughly, 'you can.'

'Please don't pretend you know me.' Her voice shook, the weight of her decision crushing down on her chest. 'Or what I'm capable of.'

'For God's sake, Jasmine!' He threw his hands up in the air. 'Don't you know how brilliant you are? You're *so* talented. And you're ready to throw it all away because why? Because you're scared? That's not good enough.'

She wanted to slap him and kiss him and be held by him. Emotion rose up within her, choking the words before they could reach her lips.

'You're better than that,' he whispered. 'Don't let your fear get the better of you.'

'Says the man who's afraid of a kiss.'

She tipped her nose up at him, forcing away the desire to lean in and kiss him. She wanted so badly for someone to comfort her. She wanted *him* to comfort her. But he'd already put that barrier firmly in place.

'Says the girl who ran away.'

CHAPTER SEVEN

A SENSE OF déjà vu washed over Jasmine as the dancers prepared for the show. She rolled her good foot around in circles, testing its flexibility, before switching to her injured ankle. It creaked under the movement but no pain materialised.

Perhaps with a little stretching she would be OK to dance the teachers' piece, especially since none of them danced *en pointe* anymore. A tiny bud of hope flickered like a flame struggling to stay alight in a draft.

What if she did dance again? Would she be able to dance outside the EJ Ballet School? Dancing *en pointe* was out of the question because her ankle was far too fragile; it was the reason her career was over. But she could move on to something else, try something new. Grant's words swirled in her head: *If you don't do it now you might not ever have the guts to perform again.*

Her palms were slick as she balled them into fists.

Could she do it? Could she step back out there and risk humiliation in front of all those people?

The first strains of the opening scene set the dancers into motion, their graceful forms taking the music and interpreting it into lyrical movement. Elise appeared beside her and patted her arm.

What if this was her last chance? The finality of such a concept made her blood run cold. What if she never danced again? She wouldn't know herself anymore. Fear lodged in her throat, its cold grip restricting her air.

You need to try again. This was the edge he'd talked about—the one where she could jump off and deal with the consequences. Or she could turn away and risk never finding her way back.

'I'm going to do it,' Jasmine whispered.

Elise grabbed her hand and squeezed. 'I knew you would.'

Intermission came and Jasmine changed into Missy's costume. She was relieved that life after ballet hadn't meant her putting on a huge amount of weight, as she'd predicted, though Missy's costume *was* still pinching her in areas. The arms and legs were too short, exposing several inches above her ankles and wrists. But it zipped up, and she could move around enough to accommodate the choreography.

If she was being honest it wasn't an ill-fitting costume that would be holding her back...

Making her way through the crowded change room, she weaved through the throng of ballet students up to the side of the stage where the teachers were waiting for her. A quick run-through of the steps would cement her decision to dance or send her into a downwards spiral of self-doubt. Either of those options was better than the purgatory of indecision that had been her life the last few months.

Elise grabbed her hand as she walked up to the wings and led her onto the stage, where the teachers were waiting. The steps came easily to her, since she'd created them, but her feet weren't as responsive as they'd used to be. A droplet of sweat ran from her hairline down the back of her neck and between her shoulderblades. She was working harder than ever before to keep up with the music. Doubt pooled in her stomach as she toiled over the repetitive *pas de chat* steps that dominated the routine.

'Stop stressing.' Elise smiled at Jasmine as she made her way off stage so the opening act of the second half could assemble. 'You created this. The rest will come naturally once you get out there.'

'I hope so.' A quiver ran through her voice. Fear was spiking her heartbeat. She rubbed the slickness of her palms down her thighs; the moisture collected a fine layer of glitter that stuck to her hands.

As the first scene of the second half played out on stage Jasmine watched with her heart in her throat. The desire to run flooded her, making her head pound and her palms itch, but she stood rooted to the ground. She wouldn't let Elise down—it was now or never.

The teachers took their place in the wings, hands interlocked across one another's bodies. Elise's hand squeezed hers as they waited. Jasmine's throat clenched as her lungs screamed for air. The dancers on stage took their finishing poses and there was silence for a brief moment before music boomed from the speakers above. She was sure everyone in the audience could hear the shaking of her breath in those few seconds.

Before she knew it she was on stage, her feet gliding in time with the music. The glare of the stage lights overwhelmed her, blinding her momentarily, until the audience came into focus. Then there was nothing but the gentle thumping of their steps as they unfolded the story. Her feet flexed and pointed, aching under the movements they were no longer used to, but she was free. With each movement a sense of abandon filled her body, running at high-speed through her veins.

As she turned the stage was a blur of shimmering particles. She had to remember to mark her spot, so she wouldn't get dizzy, but the world tilted around her in a haze of glorious fragmented light. It was unlike anything she'd felt in a long time.

They built to the climax of their performance, stepping forwards into a line of identical *arabesques*. Then the ground rushed up far too quickly. Someone gasped as Jasmine's foot released from *demi-pointe* and she fell hard into the final position. The audience applauded and the curtain dropped, but Jasmine could barely see or hear for the blinding white pain that rocketed through her.

Her ankle was on fire.

Elise lifted Jasmine's other arm over her shoulder and they carried her off stage. She put some of her weight onto her right foot and bit down on her lip, her eyes clamped shut.

'Girls, we have to keep going.' Elise shooed a startled group of dancers onto the stage in preparation for the next scene. 'Come on—we have a show to deliver.'

Jasmine limped to a chair, supported by her friends. Her ankle was already swelling and her skin had taken on a bluish hue. Her chest felt as though someone had stomped on it with a stiletto.

'Something snapped...' Her voice wavered and she swore under her breath. *No, no, no, no, no.*

'It's OK, it's probably a sprain.' Elise soothed her, her voice the epitome of cool, calm and collected. 'We need to get it elevated. Someone bring the first-aid kit.'

Jasmine clamped her eyes down in an effort to quell the pain. The commotion of the performance was a dull roar around her. Only when she heard a familiar deep baritone did she open her eyes.

'What happened?' Grant peered down at her, his brow furrowed.

'What does it look like?' she said, wincing as she tried to move her ankle. 'I proved my point.'

A group of young dancers walked past, concern for

their teacher momentarily forgotten in the presence of a footballer. Wide-eyed, they tittered behind their hands and were promptly shushed by one of the older dancers.

'What point?'

'The point where I said I couldn't dance anymore.' She sighed, closing her eyes again. 'Please go.'

'Forget it.' He crossed his arms.

She'd rather have been left alone. It was embarrassing enough that she'd injured herself on stage. She could only hope the audience hadn't noticed how hard she'd landed into the final position—perhaps they hadn't known any different. But having *him* see her at what was possibly her most vulnerable moment... Ugh, that made it a hundred times worse.

'I'm fine. Go and watch the show.' Jasmine accepted an ice pack from Elise and tried to ignore the raised eyebrows her friend was giving her. 'Honestly, I don't need any help.'

'Actually,' Elise replied, 'you probably could use Grant's help getting home. You need to keep that ankle elevated and we can't have you sitting on a rickety chair the whole night.'

Oh, no, she didn't.

'Of course,' Grant said, reaching out to Jasmine. 'I'll give you a lift.'

'No.' Jasmine swatted his hand away, mortification seeping through her as the young dancers watched the exchange. She lowered her voice. 'You've paid for your ticket; enjoy the show. Elise will take me home afterwards.'

She shot Elise a warning glance. However, she knew that once the seed of a devious idea had been planted in her best friend's mind there would be no getting away from it.

Grant knelt down in front of her and reached for the ribbons on her borrowed ballet shoe, his large hands holding her ankle as though it were a newborn duckling. His fingertips seared her skin, each delicate brush causing sensation to bloom within her.

'What are you doing?'

'There's some swelling.' He looked up at her, his cool blue eyes locked onto hers, and her stomach fluttered. He gently moved the foot, inspecting the joint for signs of a break. 'I think you'll live.'

'Of course I'll live.' She rolled her eyes and bit the words out through the pain. 'Like I said, I'm fine.'

'Jazz, you're distracting the dancers,' Elise said in a stage whisper. 'It would be best if you let Grant take you home.'

'But—'

'Go home.' Elise handed Jasmine her handbag and shooed them both, barely containing a grin. 'I'll bring your dance kit and your other bits and pieces with me later.'

A cheeky smile pulled up the edges of Grant's lips, but he kept his mouth shut. He tucked his shoulder under Jasmine's arm and helped her to her feet.

She tested pressure on her ankle and dots of white light flashed in front of her eyes.

'Ow!' A strained cry escaped her. She bit down on the fleshy part of her lower lip as pain pulsed in her ankle. The joint was on fire. Queasiness swelled in her stomach until she slumped against him, unsteady.

Jasmine hobbled out of the backstage area with Grant walking slowly beside her. Even through the pain the closeness of his body distracted her. Each slow step caused their bodies to bump against one another.

Once they were out in the hallway, and they could talk more freely, she tried to release herself from his grip. 'I can do this on my own.'

'Let me help you.'

He held her tight, but she tugged her arm from his grip. Hopping on one foot, she lifted her chin and squared her shoulders. The effect was ruined by the fact that she could only hop on her good foot.

'No.'

Letting out an exasperated sigh, he swooped down and scooped her up in his arms.

With a surprised squeak she twisted and writhed. 'Let me go!'

'Don't wriggle.'

Her face was pushed up against the hard muscle of his shoulder, her legs dangled over one of his arms and her back was cradled in the other. Every nerve-ending in her body fired warning signals. Her blood was thick and hot in her veins.

'This is absolutely ridiculous,' she muttered.

He pushed open the backstage exit with one hand and easily held her with the other. Kicking the door wide, he stepped through, making sure she didn't bump her shoulders as they exited. She'd have been impressed if she weren't so mortified.

His booming laughter filled the air, causing a few of the dance students to poke their heads out of the change room and watch as he carried her out of the building. She clutched her handbag to her chest, debating how much it would hurt if he dropped her when she brained him with it.

'This is *so* not funny.'

'No, the situation is not funny.' He made his way across the car park. 'But your cheeks are as red as tomatoes right now.'

'Way to take advantage of my predicament…'

'Trust me, if I were taking advantage of this situation you would know about it.'

If she'd been red before then what was she now? Crimson, perhaps? Her skin sizzled where it touched him, which in her current position was pretty much everywhere.

'Put me down. I can walk on my own.'

'Why can't you accept a little help?'

'Can't I be independent?' she argued. 'I don't need any-one to look after me.'

'I'd say your current situation begs to differ.'

She was losing the argument, but avoiding the question was a whole lot easier than explaining why accepting help was so painful. The moment she'd realised how much her ballet tuition was costing her parents she'd worked her ass off trying to ease their burden. But even then she'd had to do it by getting a scholarship to study at the Australian Ballet School…which was just another form of help, really.

She'd vowed as a fourteen-year-old that she would earn everything in life through her own blood, sweat and tears. She'd never be a burden on anyone ever again. But how could you say that to a guy who wanted to play big, strong rescuer?

'How far is this going to go?' she said, changing tactic.

'Don't argue with me,' he said. 'I'm taking you home.'

He didn't mean it like that, but the words sent a roaring heat to her centre all the same. Being tucked up against his broad chest with her face tilted to his neck, her lips inches from him, was oh, so tempting. She could lean in and press against the soft skin there, run her tongue along its length to see what the reaction was. To see how he tasted.

No. No, no, no. This couldn't be happening.

It had been the wrong thing to say. *I'm taking you home.*

As soon as he'd uttered the words it had been as if the floodgates had opened and in had poured all the images he'd suppressed since kissing her. Jasmine naked on top of him, under him, against the wall of the studio, laid out on the back seat of his Mercedes…

'How do you think you're going to get me home?' She interrupted his thoughts, her confidence belied by the ti-niest tremor in her voice.

'I'm going to drive.' He held her tight as she wriggled in his grip once more. Though she wasn't exactly a short woman she was light as a feather, and easy to bundle up in his arms. 'Obviously. How else would I take you home?'

'You don't know where I live.'

'You're going to tell me.'

'How do I know you're not going to take advantage of my vulnerable position?' She was stalling, the provocative question designed to make him focus on it rather than the task at hand.

However, he knew his intentions were good, and all he cared about was getting her home safely. There was nothing wrong in indulging in a little fantasy so long as he didn't act it out. The thought surprised him. It had been a long time since he'd ignored his attraction to someone. It had been longer still since he'd felt attracted enough to worry about what the other party might think.

'I'm going to set you down now.'

He stopped, lowering her gently to the ground, keeping one arm around her back so that she could lean on him and keep her weight off the injured ankle. He unlocked the car and opened the passenger-side door for her, brushing off the glitter that had transferred from her costume to his T-shirt.

She balanced on one foot, hopping away from him. 'You didn't answer my question.'

'You're in safe hands, Bun-head.' He grinned at her. 'Promise.'

'I don't know...'

She folded her arms across her chest. Her costume sparkled like a beacon under the lamps of the parking lot. She wore a funny construction in her hair that tinkled as she shook her head back and forth.

'I'm not sure I can trust you.'

He reached out and brushed his fingers through the dangling beads on her headpiece. 'Let me take you home. You have my word that I won't try to do anything untoward.'

'OK, but no judgement on my place.' She looked from the building to him and back again. 'I'm sure it's not anywhere near as fancy as yours.'

He frowned and opened his mouth to protest her lack of faith in him, but she was already hobbling towards the car. He helped her into the low bucket seat and she gave him her address to programme into his GPS.

The drive was short—a straight run down the main road from the theatre—but it was the longest fifteen minutes of his life. Being cooped up next to Jasmine and having to concentrate on the road was no mean feat. She was wound tighter than a spring by the time they pulled to a stop. Yet she'd said nothing—not even looked his way.

The trip had passed in silence. He stole a glance at her profile, illuminated in flickers by the passing street lights, but her eyes remained fixed on the road ahead.

Outside her unit, the street was quiet. No cars driving past, not a soul outside. Jasmine pushed open the door and stepped out onto the nature strip. She steadied herself on the rain-slicked ground. Grant came around the front of the car and wrapped his arms around her, hoisting her into the air as though she weighed no more than a bag of marshmallows.

'Hey, what about our deal?'

'I said I'd get you home.'

He spoke as though he had some kind of responsibility for her, provoking a sensation that felt foreign and not entirely bad.

'I *am* home.'

They made their way to her front door while she protested about how she could take care of herself. She wriggled in his grip.

'OK, OK. I'm putting you down.' He set her on the porch and she reached into her bag.

Unlocking the door, she balanced on one foot. The door swung open and she limped inside, flicking on a light. He followed her without waiting for an invitation and closed the door behind him.

'Yes, please *do* come in.'

Her voice held a hint of sarcasm that he chose to ignore. She hopped into the lounge room, her hand smoothing along the wall as she went.

'You need to get that leg up.' He followed her, making no move to leave her alone. Her face had the don't-mess-with-me look down pat, eyes narrowed.

'I'm fine,' she protested.

'Don't make me pick you up again.'

The threat hung between them, sizzling with underlying intention. Part of him was tempted to push her buttons, to see how far she would let him go. The other part—the part that smelled trouble—won over.

'Now, dinner...'

'I'm not hungry.' She hovered by the couch, running a hand over her costume to see how much glitter would transfer if she were to sit down. When her palm sparkled she remained standing. 'What I need is to get changed.'

'You need to eat. I'll order takeaway.' Pulling his mobile from the pocket of his jeans, he brought it to his ear.

She tested the back of her costume, her hands reaching behind her. Grant pretended to search for a pizza joint on his phone while watching her struggle from the corner of his eye. She switched hands and tried again.

Huffing, she conceded. 'Can you help me with this zip?'

Putting the phone down, he walked to her and she spun around, balancing on one foot. There was a long zip that ran the length of her back; she'd managed to get it down to just above where her shoulderblades were. He took the tiny puller in his hands and slowly slid it down, revealing inch after inch of flawless porcelain skin.

'Thank you,' she whispered.

A powerful urge to touch his fingertips to the subtle jut of her spine overwhelmed him. He wanted to see if she felt as silken as she looked.

Clearing his throat, he stepped back. 'No problem.'

She could hear Grant on the phone, ordering their dinner, as she hobbled to her bedroom. She felt about a million degrees in her costume, with the Lycra clinging to her body like a second, oppressive skin.

When he'd undone her zipper she'd barely been able to breathe. Her skin had cried out to have his hands brush over her, but he'd performed only his gentlemanly duties.

Sighing, she peeled the costume from her body, leaning on her bed to help keep the pressure off her injured ankle. The throbbing had quietened, and she knew from experience it wasn't a serious injury. Still, she'd learned her lesson about returning to the stage. That dream would go back into the dark recesses of her heart for a while…at least until she'd forgotten the sting of humiliation enough to contemplate trying again.

She changed into sweat pants and a T-shirt, making certain to pick the ones that hugged her closely without looking as if she'd chosen them on purpose. She made her way back out to the main room in time to hear Grant in the kitchen.

'What are you looking for?' And why was he going through her cupboards? He was certainly acting familiar for someone who had entered her home for this first time.

Grant came back to the lounge with a tall glass of water. 'I've got some anti-inflammatories in my bag if you want?'

'No, thank you.' She reached for the water and sipped, watching him warily as he dropped down onto the couch opposite her. His legs were too long for the crowded space of her unit; he bent his knees and let them fall apart. The position was unabashedly male, and Jasmine had to divert her eyes or else she'd be staring straight at his crotch.

By the time the pizza arrived she was starving. Though she wouldn't admit it to Grant, the thought of hot melted cheese and carbs was far better than anything she could have whipped up in her ill-equipped kitchen. He answered the door and paid for their dinner. The steaming box was making her stomach churn in anticipation.

She shuffled over on the couch to make room, so that they could share the pizza from the same box.

'Are you going to get back on the horse?'

'You don't beat around the bush, do you?'

She rolled her eyes, swiping a slice from the box and biting into it. Tangy parmesan cheese melded with salty olives and spicy salami on her tongue. It wasn't ordinary pizza—this was the good stuff...the proper Italian stuff. She stifled a moan of pleasure. The man knew his food.

'It's a waste of time. If I have a question, I ask it.' He chewed. 'Simple.'

'I don't know...sometimes I think maybe I should take the hint.'

'What hint?'

'That it's over—that part of my life, I mean.' She shrugged. Now that she'd got home and her ankle had eased she'd calmed down. But the thought of getting back out on stage was, for the moment, stuck in the 'crap to deal with another day' basket.

'You shouldn't give up.'

'Ah, well, if it's that simple, then...'

'It is.' He reached for another slice and closed the lid of the pizza box. 'If you're passionate about it then you put up with the bad bits.'

'Do you ever think about doing anything else aside from footy?'

'Not really.' He looked thoughtful. 'Well, I studied psychology at university, but I haven't done anything with it.'

Jasmine couldn't help the quirk of her eyebrows.

'Don't look so shocked,' he said, frowning at her. 'We're not all dumb jocks, you know.'

'No judgement here.' She reached for another slice. 'I just figured that it seemed unlikely that you were lucky enough to be a professional athlete, look the way you do and be smart as well. You have to admit that's kind of lucky.'

'Have you forgotten the Rubik's cube story already?' He grinned, a small spot of tomato sauce clinging to the corner of his lip. 'And what do you mean by "look the way you do"?'

She sucked in a breath; the words had tumbled out uncensored. Clearly her guard had dropped while she'd been stuffing her face with pizza.

'Well, at the moment you look like a bit of a grub,' she said, her belly curling anxiously.

He swiped his tongue along the edge of his lip, catching the sauce and grinning, as though he knew exactly how hot she was burning inside.

'I want you to promise me something.' His tone changed, and his brow narrowed above an intent stare. 'Don't let this beat you.'

She wasn't ready to go there yet. She wasn't ready to have this conversation…especially not with him.

'Grant…' Her voice issued a warning, but he would not be deterred.

'I meant everything I said before you stepped out on that stage.' He swallowed. 'This is a stumbling block, not the end of the road. Your ankle will be fine in a week or so, and I want you to keep trying.'

'I don't want to talk about this.' She felt hot, angry tears pricking at her eyes. She would not break down in front of him. This was *her* pain. Hers alone.

'You need to talk.' His hand was on her arm, stroking the length from her shoulder to her elbow in deep, reassuring lines. 'It'll help you get past it.'

'Is that your psychology degree talking?'

'It's someone who cares talking.'

'Why do you care?'

She wasn't sure she wanted to know the answer. The feelings that had been bubbling below the surface—the attraction, the desire and the inkling of something more—were things she didn't have room for...or, more truthfully, didn't have the guts for.

'Because you're crazy-talented, and smart and...different.' Something flickered across his face—realisation, perhaps?

'*Different* is usually a synonym for something negative,' she pointed out, trying to lighten the mood.

'But you *are* different—to me at least. Do you know this is the most conversation I've exchanged with a woman in...God, I can't even remember.'

'Are you usually too busy getting to business with most women?'

He raked a hand through his hair, the gold strands catching the soft glow of the lamp. 'Something like that.'

'Don't you talk to your mum?' She tilted her head, suddenly curious beyond belief about this secretive man in front of her.

'Actually, no. Mum hasn't been with us for some time.'

'I'm so sorry.' She bit her lip.

'The whole family thing is...strained.' His mouth drew into a flat line. 'I guess some families aren't meant to be close.'

Her mind flashed to her mother and father. It had been

a while since she'd seen them. Facing them was harder these days. The worry on her mother's face or in her tone on the voice mails she left made her chest ache. Guilt was an ugly, dirty, painful emotion.

'Are you close with your folks?' Grant peered at her as though trying to see exactly what was going on in her head.

'Not as much as I should be.'

'Are they far away?'

'About forty-five minutes.' She smiled ruefully. 'Not far enough for me to claim it as an excuse. I haven't seen them much since the accident.'

'Why?'

'It's hard. They sacrificed a lot to enable me to dance, and look what I've done with it…'

'I'm sure they don't blame you.'

'They don't.'

They'd been by her side all through the surgery, the rehabilitation, her return to the company… It had only been after she'd quit her position with the Australian Ballet that it had become hard to look them in the eye.

'But you still feel guilty?'

'Ashamed is probably more accurate.' She sighed. 'I call my mum every week, but I have to force myself to do it. Sometimes I'd rather curl up in a corner and ignore the world.'

'You have *nothing* to be ashamed of.'

'I poured every cent they spent on my ballet tuition down the drain when I crashed that car. I guess it's lucky that I managed to get a scholarship when I started training seriously, so at least I didn't send them completely broke in the process.'

Hands shaking, she reached for another slice of pizza, determined to give her mouth something to do instead of spilling out her skeletons to Grant. He did the same and they ate in silence.

'You don't have to throw it all away,' he said. 'You *can* dance again. Maybe not ballet, but I'm sure there are other types of dance that you could do. Surely your training would help?'

'Why do you believe that I'm such a great dancer? You've never seen what I was like before…'

'I've seen your eyes when you dance, your face. That tells me enough.'

He had another droplet of sauce on the corner of his mouth. She reached her hand to his lips and wiped the spot, her fingertips grazing his skin.

He caught her wrist in his hand, bringing it to his mouth and slowly drawing her in. As he wrapped his lips around her finger and sucked Jasmine's heart stilled. The gentle pressure made her throb, and a jolt of arousal ran through her.

As he released her their wide-eyed gazes mirrored one another. She drew her hand back, holding it to her chest as the finger burned where he'd tasted her. Neither of them moved.

The silence between them was thick, heavy. Grant's eyes were clouded, his pupils dilated with the lust he held back. Silent tension pushed and pulled, threatening to shatter their restraint.

'I should go.'

His voice was heavy, each word rough with desire as he leant back, creating more distance between them…as if that would help.

'Why don't you stay?'

Was she doing this? Her voice had been the merest of whispers, barely audible above the sound of her fluttering heart.

Torment seeped into his features. His mouth pulled into a firm line and he looked at her.

'I shouldn't…'

And yet he lingered. He was inches from her; she could reach out and touch him, reach out and shatter those last shards of control with a gentle brush of her fingertips. She knew she had it in her to be sensual again, to use her body for pleasure.

She placed her hand on his denim-clad thigh and smoothed the fabric beneath her fingertips. Hard muscle flexed beneath her touch and she could swear all his breath rushed out into the air between them. She leant forwards, her lips parted.

Two solid hands eased her back against the couch, and when the pressure of his body didn't follow Jasmine's eyes snapped open. Grant was on his feet, looking down to where she sat.

'I'm not starting something that neither of us will be able to stop.'

'What if I don't want to stop it?' Humiliation burned beneath her skin but she had to ask—she had to know how he felt.

'That's exactly what I'm trying to avoid.'

She didn't move her gaze from the floor until the front door clicked behind him. Only then did she let herself dissolve.

CHAPTER EIGHT

GRANT WOKE UP with grit in his eyes. Yet another night of inadequate sleep, though this time it hadn't been due to the nightmares. This time his mind had been occupied with dreams of another kind.

Dreams of Jasmine sprawled beneath him on her couch, pressed up against the railing of his balcony, on her coffee table… The list went on. He was finding it harder and harder to resist her charms, and when she'd reached for him last night—when she'd asked him to stay—it had taken every last morsel of will to keep from ravishing her on the spot.

He thumped the tiled wall of the shower, releasing a fraction of his pent-up frustration. It wouldn't do. He'd had a cold shower as soon as he'd arrived home last night and yet he'd still woken up with a raging hard-on and a head full of fantasies. She'd dug herself so far under his skin that he didn't know left from right. Even when he promised himself he'd leave her alone, he couldn't stay away!

The hot water rushed over him as he pressed his forehead against the tiles so the back of his neck was under the strongest part of the stream. He rolled his shoulders and groaned. No matter what he did, no matter how he rationalised away his attraction to Jasmine, she managed to throw it all out of the window with a single look.

'Dammit,' he growled against the wall.

With a flick of his wrist he shut down the hot water and flinched as an icy stream hit him dead-on. The cold water stung his body but it would quash his excitement... for now. At least until the next time he saw her.

Grant stepped out of the shower and wrapped himself in a big fluffy towel. He wandered into the lounge room and turned on the TV. While he fired up his coffee machine he heard someone saying his name. He turned in time to catch the daytime entertainment reporter for Channel 9.

'It's been a while since we've seen footy players behaving *this* badly.' Her exaggerated facial expressions made him curl his lip into a sneer. 'But I'm sure you'll all remember when Grant Farley, full forward for the Vic Harbour Jaguars, had a *very* public fall from grace last year.'

His photo flashed up onto the screen. He had a fat lip, from the one punch he hadn't been able to dodge, and his eyes were bloodshot beyond recognition. He was barely standing.

'After spending the night in prison he was charged for starting a brawl that landed two men in hospital. Luckily for Grant the assault charges were dropped shortly after. I guess that's what happens when you're one of the highest earners in the AFL.'

Her perky voice dipped an octave as she leant in close to the camera, the screen capturing her ample cleavage.

'Now, this week's mugshot comes from star—'

Grant switched off the TV, his blood boiling. It had been a year. A whole damn year and they were still feeding off his photo like a pack of vultures. Shame washed over him, as it did every time he was reminded of when he'd hit rock bottom.

His partying had got steadily worse through his mid-twenties, and then he'd started blacking out and getting into trouble.

The night it had all come to a head he'd drunk so much

that he hadn't been able to do more than throw the first punch before his friends had jumped in and he'd stumbled off. The pub's security system had shown clearly that he hadn't thrown any of the blows that landed the two men in hospital. Still, he'd been the only famous one there, and he had deep pockets.

Grant had never felt lower than when he'd signed that cheque to make it all go away. He'd taken voluntarily leave from the club so they didn't get dragged down with him. He'd disappeared overseas for a few months, cleared his head and come back with the strongest commitment of his life—the commitment to do right by his club and his fans.

It had been a whole year, he hadn't gone clubbing once, and his career was back on track. He'd also ditched the so-called best friend who had leaked the photo to the media, making a promise to himself that no one would ever use him again.

However, the media loved to tell his story over and over. He wondered how long it would be before they forgot about it—if they ever did. What if he could never clear the mud from his name?

He cringed; the Farley name had been an honourable one once. The rural veterinary and farming business his father ran had had a good, solid reputation in their community... Now they were known as the family whose son had gone off the rails. It was an inerasable mistake—one that had cost him dearly.

Maybe if he could get one win this season he could prove he was back on track. At least then he'd have the respect of the fans and of his team. That would be a step in the right direction.

Jasmine had been cooped up inside for days since her fall. Her ankle was looking better: the swelling had reduced and the bruises had shifted from purple to a yellowish-brown. It wasn't a pretty sight, but it was a far cry from what she'd feared.

She knew the drill—take it easy, give the strain time to heal, keep the ankle elevated. But she was bored, bored, *bored*.

The drivel they featured on daytime TV didn't hold her interest and she'd devoured three books from cover to cover before exhausting her supply of new reading material. She needed something to distract her—anything to take her mind off the shambles that Grant Farley had made of her senses.

Jasmine huffed, resting against the side of her couch while she looked around, desperate for something to do. All she could think about was how close she'd come to letting him in, to baring herself and all her flaws to a man she barely knew. It was stupid. Reckless.

The last time she'd trusted a man she'd flushed her career down the toilet. Kyle hadn't come to visit her once after her surgery, though she'd heard reports that he'd used his social rank—and the donations his family had made to the hospital—to check in with her doctor as to the status of her injuries. It had been concluded that she wouldn't be dancing for a very long time, if ever again.

After that there had been a brief note delivered by one of the hospital staff. His elegant handwriting had told her that their relationship wouldn't work out. And that had been that. She'd never seen him again.

The humiliation still burned in her throat every time she thought of the absolute car crash—no pun intended—that had been her relationship with Kyle Waterhouse. Not only had he treated her as the ultimate asset—something to show off to his mates as a sign of his status—but he'd viewed her very much in the same way as the projects and stocks he funded. She was something to throw money at, to control and shape as he pleased. He had not cared about her beyond potential returns. And when she'd no longer been valuable he'd cut his losses.

Tears prickled behind her eyelids, hot and angry. She couldn't stay cooped up in this house any longer, lest she send herself around the twist. Though she wasn't supposed to drive, Elise's mother's car was automatic and her good foot was the only one she needed. Surely a little trip to the ballet studio wouldn't hurt? It wasn't far from home and the fresh air would do her good.

Besides, she wanted to find out how the rest of the performance had gone and to see if any of her students had been approached by the scouts. Feeling justified, she stood and limped to the car.

By the time Jasmine pulled the car into the studio's parking lot her ankle was burning. She pushed herself from the seat, balancing on her good leg. The walk to the studio door seemed to take for ever as she alternated between limping and hopping. All the while she cursed herself for not bringing the crutches Dr Wilson had lent her.

'What are you doing here?' Elise abandoned her choreography midstep to admonish Jasmine as she hobbled into the studio.

'I couldn't stay at home, El. I was going crazy.' She hopped in a pitiful little circle. 'See? I'm fine.'

Elise shook her head but she didn't argue. 'I'll get you a chair.'

Dragging one from the reception desk, she placed it at the front of the studio. Grateful, Jasmine dropped down and settled in to watch the class.

As they were wrapping up Jasmine noticed Grant had arrived for his lesson. Given her state of relative immobility—not that she was allowing herself to be confined by it—Elise had offered to cover her lessons for the week without taking any money. Lucky, since Jasmine was walking a fine line between making ends meet and having her phone cut off.

Grant walked into the studio and came straight up to Jasmine. Lines creased his forehead and his strong jaw was set into a forbidding angle.

'You're supposed to be resting.' He stood over her, arms folded across his chest so that his biceps bulged beneath his T-shirt. His full lips pursed into a shape far more appealing than it should have been, given he was admonishing her as one might a child.

Jasmine shrugged. 'It's boring.'

He tilted his head to one side and gave her an impatient look. 'That's a pretty weak excuse.'

'Consider yourself lucky you got one at all.'

He sighed. 'You should be resting.'

'You said that already.'

They stared at one another, the air crackling between them. Part of Jasmine knew he was right, but the other part wanted to give him a kick in the shins for being so bossy. Since he'd rejected her advance the other night she knew the smart move would be to push him away.

'When you two are done I'll start the lesson.' Elise stood in the middle of the studio with her hands on her hips.

She pulled a stern face but Jasmine could see the amused smile twitching on the edge of her lips.

'Wait around and I'll take you home afterwards.' He turned to meet Elise.

'My car is here,' she protested. 'I don't need you to chauffeur me around.'

'It wasn't a question.'

Grant knew he was pushing the boundaries with Jasmine, but the girl didn't seem to want to take care of herself. She had a self-destructive streak that unnerved him—

probably because he'd seen that same capacity in himself. And learning she was the one who'd caused her accident had only made him more certain she needed someone to look after her. Elise seemed to keep an eye out, but he doubted that was enough.

When he'd gone through the kitchen cupboards at her house he'd noticed how bare they were: a whole lot of tea and coffee, a few muesli bars and some limp-looking fruit and veggies in her fridge. Not the kind of nutrition required for someone who had a physical job like she did.

She sighed, but didn't make a move to leave. Instead she stayed in the chair and watched as Elise began her instruction.

He was finding it difficult to concentrate on Elise's voice because his mind kept wandering to Jasmine. She watched them with an open interest, and he felt the weight of her stare on his shoulders. He was messing up the steps and growing increasingly frustrated with the exercises.

The lesson was a disaster. In truth, he was completely over the ballet treatment thing, but something urged him to continue...and it wasn't the benefits his hamstring was seeing.

'Tough lesson?' Jasmine asked as he came up to her afterwards. Her head tilted to the side, sending dark, glossy hair slipping over her shoulder. She looked delectable, even free of make-up and dressed in jeans and a grey sweater.

'Tough when you were staring me down.'

'I wasn't staring you down.' She laughed, pushing up onto her good leg. 'You seem to get off on the knight in shining armour thing, so I'll let you take me home tonight but that's it. Tomorrow I go back to looking after myself, OK?'

'We'll see,' he grumbled. He wrapped his arm around her waist and pulled her to him so he could help her to the door.

'I *am* going to remind you that this is completely unnecessary,' she said, looking up at him. 'I drove myself here.'

'Just because you did doesn't mean you should have.'

Her body fitted perfectly against his, and it was tough for him not to notice that as she made a lame attempt to get rid of him. As she hopped her shoulder bumped against him, her hand tightening around his lower back. It was all he needed to imagine where else he'd like those hands to be on him...smoothing over his chest, cupping his ass and—

'Good night, you two.'

Elise's sing-song voice caused Jasmine to turn around and glare at her friend. Her cheeks coloured to a faint pink, making his pulse race even more.

'You know I'm going to have to come back here in the morning and collect the car.' Jasmine sighed as he helped her out of the studio and towards the Mercedes.

'I'll have it brought to your unit.' He wasn't going to let her make her way home on her own—not with an injured foot on these icy roads. If something happened to her he would never forgive himself.

Grant frowned. He wasn't sure what it was about Jasmine that was stirring all these protective instincts. The only woman he'd ever cared to protect had been Chelsea, and look how that had turned out.

'OK, fine.'

He held the door open for her and she slid awkwardly into his car. When he was satisfied she was OK he walked around to the driver's side and got in. Firing up the engine, he let the car warm up before backing it out.

'So what's the deal with you wanting to look after me?' Jasmine watched him closely as she questioned him, her eyes narrowed slighly. 'Do you have some compelling need to protect women you barely know?'

'I know you.'

She paused for a moment. 'No, you don't.'

'Yes, I do.' He glanced sideways at her. 'I know you're a great dancer who's trapped because of a stupid mistake.'

'I don't know if my most recent performance would allow anyone to classify me as a great dancer.' She bit down on her lower lip.

'I know you like to be in control and you hate asking for help. I know that Elise is pretty much the only person you have in your life.'

Jasmine blinked, her eyebrows arched. 'OK, so maybe you know me a bit.'

'I studied psychology at university, remember? I can read people.'

'So what are you reading now?'

'You're testing me, although I'm not sure why.' Grant forced away a smile at her open-mouthed surprise, though he could hardly claim much achievement in accurately assessing her—reading her face was as easy as reading a book.

'OK, that's kind of freaky.'

'Why don't you fill in the blanks, then?'

'I don't know why I'd do that,' she said, her voice small. She was looking out of the window, avoiding him. 'I'm not ready for this. But I can't seem to push you away... I don't think I want to.'

The honesty of her statement was a fist to his stomach. She felt the same way he did. They were two people who knew better, who were smart, who protected themselves from all the crap that life threw at them. Yet neither of them could resist the gravitational pull when they were together. It relieved him to know that she felt it too.

'I don't know what I'm doing,' she continued. 'But I can't stop wanting to touch you, wanting to taste you.'

His lips ran dry at her last statement, his tongue heavy in his mouth as he steadied his breath. His blood seemed to pulse twice as fast as he looked at her, his flickering glance capturing the flush of her pale skin under the streetlamps. The arousal he'd been fighting pooled in his groin and desire wrenched inside him.

'It's strange, I haven't felt this kind of attraction to anyone in a long time...not since the accident.'

'Why are you telling me all this?'

'I thought you wanted to know.'

The uncertainty in her voice almost broke him in two. He wanted to hold her and tell her everything would be OK.

'I do.'

'It must be your psychology voodoo.'

'Yeah, that must be it.'

He laughed and she offered up a small smile. It was like a peek of sunshine through storm clouds—a sliver of hope against the grey backdrop of her fear.

Neither of them spoke while they lost themselves in their thoughts. They were both damaged goods, victims of broken hearts, and casualties of laying yourself bare to another human being.

He'd promised himself he would never go there again, but it was getting harder and harder to ignore the way she awakened him. She stirred the old Grant—the one who loved without fear. He felt a spark of his former self, the wide-eyed kid from the country who'd wanted to study psychology because he had a burning to desire to help people, to know more about them, to unravel them until he understood what made them tick. It was a part of him long dead and buried.

Now he pushed people away as a default. But she made him want to reach out again. She made him want to crawl out of his cave.

'What happened wasn't your fault.' His voice cracked as he tried to console her.

'Yes, it was.' She nodded, the look of resignation on

her face one he suspected she'd worn many times before. 'I drank the champagne, I got into the car and I hit the accelerator. That makes it my fault.'

'I don't mean that.' He shook his head. 'I mean the way he treated you. *That* wasn't your fault.'

'I used him as much as he used me.' She laughed, the sound hollow and sharp in his ears. 'He used me because he liked having a pretty thing on his arm, and I liked him because he got me more face-time with directors.'

'I'm sure you didn't need it.'

'I didn't,' she said, her voice wavering. 'But I was so insecure back then, and I didn't realise he'd been feeding me lies to keep me close to him. He made me believe that I wasn't able to make it on my own, that I wouldn't succeed without his help.'

Her mouth drew into a grim line. Her regret was palpable in the air.

Grant pulled up in front of her house and turned off the engine. She wouldn't meet his eyes, looking down so that all he could see were the tops of the dark curly lashes that framed them. In a moment of impulse he reached out and cupped her cheeks with his hands. They seemed so large in comparison to her small, delicate features.

'Look at me,' he commanded.

Her eyes flickered up and they sat there for a moment, unmoving in the darkness of the car. He knew he shouldn't, he knew it was the wrong thing to do by her...by them both...but that didn't stop the intensity with which he brought his lips down to hers.

There was nothing tentative about his kiss, no gentle exploring of her. It was hungry and raw. It took her a moment to respond, but when she did it was with equal fervour. Her small rosebud mouth opened up to him, her tongue meeting his. He could taste the honeyed sweetness of her, smell the faded soap on her skin.

His senses sparked and flared as he drank her in: taste, smell, touch…and sound. A small moan escaped her mouth when he ran his hand down from her face to her shoulders, down her arms, grazing her breasts as he went. The soft fabric of her sweater showed no resistance to his touch.

Outside the car a dog barked and the lights of a lone car passing by broke them apart. The car was cooling down and Jasmine shivered next to him.

'Let me get you inside.' His voice was hoarse, barely recognisable through the haze of lust that roughened its edges.

Jasmine nodded. Her lips were puffy from the roughness of his kiss, her cheeks pink, her eyes wide. She opened the door but waited for him to help her, for once. He darted around to the passenger side and reached down to help her out of the car. She gripped his arm and steadied herself on her good foot as she rose slowly from the low seat on the passenger side.

Sliding an arm around her waist, he leant down and kissed her again. Her back pressed against the car, his hips pinning her down. He found her mouth, hot and ready for him this time. Hands came to his hair; her fingers tangling in the lengths of it, tugging it. Showing him that he wasn't in charge.

Though she came close to matching him in height, she still felt tiny next to him. Her long, slender arms and graceful dancer's legs were easily pinned down by his strength, though as she pressed against him now he knew that she wouldn't be delicate in bed.

He swallowed and pulled away, looking down at her soulful brown eyes as they glowed at him from under the streetlamp. Her lips were parted and she dragged her bottom lip between her teeth. He knew where this was going.

This was his last chance; he could turn away now and protect her. He could protect his heart from being shattered again. He felt as if time was standing still as he deliberated, his head pulling him away and his body pushing him closer.

He should leave. She deserved someone who could take better care of her than he could...

'Grant...' she whispered, and his name sounded like a plea on her lips. 'Take me inside. Please.'

And with that the very last scraps of his resolve were shattered. He scooped her up and she immediately wound her arms around his neck—no protest this time. In a few strides he crossed the front yard and set her down so that she could open the front door. He hugged her from behind while she fiddled with the lock, his hands slipping under the hem of her jumper to find the bare skin of her belly. It was smooth and flat, her skin hot to the touch despite the cold outside.

The door finally opened and she limped inside with him close behind her, pulling the door shut. The unit was cold. Jasmine turned on the heater from a panel in the entrance.

'We don't need that,' he said, coming up behind her and bringing his lips down to her neck.

She simmered beneath him, her hips tilting backwards so that she could press her ass against him.

'It's going to get hot in here.'

CHAPTER NINE

GRANT REACHED FOR Jasmine and scooped her up. She felt slightly ridiculous, with him carrying her everywhere, but as his mouth met hers again she lost herself in the velvet warmth of his kiss.

'Which way?' He murmured his question against her lips.

She motioned to the bedroom, her response muffled against him. He nudged the door open with his foot, carrying her through before setting her gently down in front of him. She balanced on one foot and encircled his neck with her arms, dragging him down for another searing kiss.

A snake-like sensation twisted and turned in her gut. It had been so long since she'd had sex—not since breaking up with Kyle, though his frequent infidelities had meant their sex life had died a while before that fateful night.

What if she'd forgotten how to seduce? How to pleasure? How to enjoy her body?

She ignored the fluttering of her heart and the prickling of her palms. She needed this—she needed to be loved in a physical sense. She'd been deprived for so long and there would be no fighting it.

Leaning down to plant a soft kiss on his mouth, she sucked in a breath. Her tongue brushed over his lower lip in a sweet, tentative stroke, eliciting a groan. She had him right where she wanted him, so hungry with desire he was unlikely to notice or care about her leg.

He grasped the hem of her sweater and pulled it up slowly. Her T-shirt followed and then she was wearing only her jeans and the lacy blush-pink bra she'd thought nothing of wearing that morning. It looked sensual against her skin; she'd always had a thing for beautiful lingerie and her drawers were filled with a rainbow of lacy, frilly French things. It seemed he too enjoyed them—his eyes drank her in as though she were the proverbial glass of water on a hot summer's day.

'I don't expect anything out of this.' Her voice shook as he traced the scalloped edge of the bra with his fingertip.

'Me neither.'

'I mean, I'm not looking for anything permanent right now.'

He dragged his gaze away from her breasts, the endless depths of his sky-blue eyes drawing her in and yet telling her nothing. His face was unreadable except for the arousal that widened his pupils, simmering below the surface.

'Nor am I.'

'One night only,' she whispered, knowing full well that words alone couldn't protect her. She was in too deep and her heart was desperately trying to maintain the distance that her body was unable to. But the words were hollow. Meaningless. He was under her skin and one night would never be enough.

'No one gets hurt.' He brushed the edge of her jaw with his hand, tilting her face.

'No one gets hurt,' she echoed.

Grant's hands dropped to her waist, undoing the zip on her jeans, and then he was bending down, dragging the denim with him as he went. Her French knickers in baby-blue cotton were trimmed with the same blush-pink lace as her bra.

He sighed, and the slow whoosh of breath tickled the exposed skin of her thighs. He traced a line of kisses along the edge of her underwear, sending goosebumps rippling across her skin. She removed her sneakers and leant on him, stepping out of her jeans gingerly to avoid putting too much pressure on her sprained ankle. He reached for the top of the knee-high white cotton socks she wore to keep her legs warm…and to hide the scars.

'Don't,' she whispered. 'Leave them on.'

She couldn't do it. No matter how hungry he got he wouldn't be able to ignore the puckered flesh and shades of red. She knew that.

Distract him—quickly!

She loosened her hair from the tie that held it in place so that the dark strands tumbled over her shoulders and bust. She tossed the tie to one side, not even looking to see where it landed. Giving her head a little shake, she felt her hair fall about her.

'Holy hell.' His mouth formed an appreciative O. 'I can honestly say I've never seen a more exciting sight in all my life.'

'Is that so?' She cocked her head to the side, allowing her hair to brush over her hardened nipples as they pressed against the lacy fabric that contained them. A tight clenching sensation in her stomach sent heat spiralling down to the juncture of her thighs.

'You've knocked finals off the top of the list.'

He reached for her, drawing her waist to him with one hand and using his other to gather her hair and pull it over her shoulders. It slipped down her back, the ends tickling the bare patch of skin above the waistband of her French knickers.

'No other woman has ever come close to that.'

'I'm sure I'm not like the girls you're used to,' she said, her voice raspy and low.

She was shaking on the inside. His reaction excited and terrified her. She knew he would be a practised lover, far more experienced than her, and she could only hope it wouldn't show.

He ran a fingertip over her collarbone before dropping his hand to cup her breast, his thumb and forefinger gently rolling a taut nipple through the thin fabric. 'You're nothing like anything I've ever experienced before.'

Jasmine's head rolled back as pleasure shot through her veins, heating every inch of her body in rapid succession. Grant's touch was equal parts gentle and insistent, his expert movements slowly eroding her fear. If she didn't have him soon she'd burst.

She reached for the hem on his jumper and pulled it off—along with his T-shirt—in one swift movement. He was the perfect specimen of male health, muscular and lean. She ran her hands down the front of his chest, admiring the freckles that scattered across his skin to where his tattoos finished. The colourful intricate lines spread up towards his shoulder and down over the top of his arm. She traced the outline of the psi symbol woven into the design. Running her hands down his chest, she brushed her finger over his nipples and continued down to the waistband of his pants.

Hovering, her hands trembled above the tell-tale bulge of his excitement. She hooked a finger under the waistband of his pants and brushed the taut skin there. A shudder rippled through him as her hands continued their exploration, coaxing him gently as she went.

'Good Lord, you're a tease.' A frustrated growl rumbled low in his throat. He pulled her to him, cupping her buttocks with both hands so that she was pressed against him as hard as possible. And hard he was, the thick length of him digging into her lower belly.

Without warning Grant leant forwards and scooped

Jasmine up, her legs dangling over one of his arms as she wound her own arms around his neck for support. Their lips met as he walked to her bed, and her hands found themselves once again amidst the thick mass of his golden hair. His mouth was urgent now, lips rough and probing against hers.

Dropping her to the bed, Grant stripped completely to reveal the full extent of his arousal. Reaching for him, she felt her breath catch in her throat. Her fingertips brushed the silky strength of his erection. He was magnificent. Hotter than anything she could have dreamed up on the nights she spent alone in this very bed.

'I need you, Grant,' she whispered, grabbing his hips and pulling him down to her. 'I need you inside me.'

'Not yet.' His lips skimmed over hers and found their resting place around a tight, sensitive nipple. He pushed the strap of her bra down so that he could remove her breast from its delicate confines. Jasmine's back arched at the sudden intensity of pleasure that pooled within her. His tongue flicked against the sensitive bud, heightening her excitement so that behind her closed lids all she could focus on was the heat of his mouth on her.

His hand trailed down the plane of her stomach, dancing lightly over the lacy knickers to her bare knee above one of her socks. He smoothed his hand back up, letting his fingers skirt the edge of her underwear. He let out a throaty laugh against her breast as she squirmed beneath him.

'Who's the tease now?' she panted, gripping the bedspread and bunching the thick material in her hands.

With continued gentleness he kissed his way to her other breast and removed her bra altogether. Discarding the scrap of lace with one hand, he toyed with the scalloped edge of her knickers near her inner thigh. Jasmine gasped as his fingers brushed over her sex. She'd reached boiling point, her blood simmering while he stoked the fire within her. He touched her with an unhurried enjoyment, each stroke, kiss, lick doled out with a lazy sensuality that made her head spin.

He peeled back the waistband of her kickers and removed them slowly, all the while watching as he revealed her inch by inch.

'Stunning,' he murmured.

As he lay down beside her Grant possessed her mouth, leaving her dizzy through lack of air. He dipped a finger into her core, rubbing his thumb gently across the tight bud at her centre. Jasmine let out a cry. His teasing had wound her tighter than she'd ever experienced. Tighter than she'd thought possible. Her body ascended slowly to climax and she revelled in the exquisite torture of pleasure a hair's breadth out of reach.

'Please, Grant.' She grabbed his face with her hands, forcing him to look at her. 'Don't make me wait.'

Jasmine reached over to the drawer in her nightstand and fished around for a condom. There had to be one in there—surely she hadn't thrown them all out. Her fingers moved about the drawer as the sound of their breathing filled the air.

Please.

Mercifully, her fingers brushed the crinkled edges of a condom packet. She handed it to Grant and he tore it open. Lying back, Jasmine felt her stomach flutter with anticipation as he took care of their protection. He paused before slowly lowering himself to her, nudging her legs apart with his thighs.

His hands were on either side of her, his face hovering above hers. At this angle his golden hair flopped forwards, the too-long ends brushing his forehead. She'd never wanted a man so badly as she wanted him right now.

She bit down on her lower lip as he filled her completely, the sensation sucking the air from her lungs. She adjusted to the thickness of him and his face burrowed against her neck. The weight of him pressing her into the bed was exquisite—terrifying and all-consuming.

'Jasmine...' he groaned. 'You're so damn...'

He trailed off as he moved inside her, slowly at first, giving her time to adjust. His hands roamed her, stroking up and down the lengths of her arms, tangling themselves in her hair, cupping the sides of her face as he kissed her. Gathering speed, he bucked his hips against her hot, wet centre. She tilted to meet his thrusts, giving him greater access. Complete access.

He slipped one arm beneath her lower back, drawing her body to his as he pushed back onto his knees and pulled her up so that she straddled him. He bore the weight of her and she moved her leg so that there was no pressure on her ankle.

Upright, Jasmine was exposed as she met him eye to eye. From her vantage point she could watch everything about their lovemaking, from the stark contrast of his tanned, freckled skin against the porcelain of hers to the way his shoulders tensed as she rode him. His eyes were half open, heavy-lidded with desire, and his thick lashes fluttered as she moved her hips in a circular motion.

She lowered her head and pressed her lips to his shoulder as she leant against him, her breasts flattened against his chest. They were fused, moving with a harmony she'd never experienced before. Perhaps this was the way it felt when there was no agenda other than lust.

He ran his hands up and down her sock-covered legs. Her breath caught as his fingers brushed over where her scars were hidden beneath nylon and cotton. She studied his face for any change but he appeared not to have noticed. Relaxing, she brought her face to his and planted a hot, open-mouthed kiss on his lips. He tasted mildly salty from where a thin sheen of sweat coated his upper lip. Responding immediately, he kissed her back with force until her lips were bruised and puffy.

He shifted to be properly beneath her, while she writhed on top of him. She felt incredible, with the blatant adoration in his eyes urging her on, urging her to open up to him. She ran her palms over her body while she continued circling her hips, brushing her hands over her own breasts and flicking her hair over her shoulder so that it dropped down to where his legs extended underneath her.

The tension rose. He gripped her, urging an increase in speed. She held him back, teasing him until the last possible moment, dangling the possibility of release over him like a taunt.

But it seemed Grant had other plans. He slipped a hand between them and a sharp jolt of pleasure ripped through her as his thumb connected with her clitoris. He massaged the swollen bud until she was panting. Her breath came in short bursts as she climbed higher and higher. She clenched around him as waves of pleasure rolled through her.

Her climax came hard and fast, causing her to clamp her eyes shut. It felt as if she was bursting apart at the seams. Her whole body shuddered with release and she gripped him so hard she thought she might break him in two. She opened her eyes to stare straight into Grant's, pushing her hair from her face as she smiled at him.

'That was…' she said, still catching her breath. 'Something else.' She pressed her lips to his neck, grazing her teeth along the roped muscles. He smelled faintly of aftershave—something woody and earthy. She breathed it in as she murmured, 'Come for me.'

The words pushed Grant over the edge; he gripped her hips and increased their rhythm so that he could tip himself into oblivion. He cried out her name as he came, his face contorted with ecstasy, and then he fell back against the pillow, sated.

Jasmine watched Grant, and instead of removing herself from him lay down so her body was flat against his. His heart thudded against her chest and the deepness of his breath blew warm on her ear. He let out a mumble of enjoyment as he pressed his lips to her temple.

'*You're* something else.' Their faces were so close that his eyelashes brushed her cheek.

Jasmine's chest contracted and pleasure tugged in response to his praise. She'd never felt like this after sex—she'd never felt this deep bonding and connection with another. It was as though she was safe, as if she was even and equal with him.

One night only—that was the deal.

She couldn't deny the comfort of lying on top of Grant now, and nor could she deny the way her body sang out when he wrapped his strong, thick arms around her. His fingertips traced the lines of her back, causing little ripples of pleasure to run through her.

Against her better judgement, Jasmine wished that time would stand still so she could savour her body against his.

What a day. He'd gone from ignoring thoughts of the lithe ballet teacher to experiencing her first-hand. Pushing guilty thoughts from his mind, he watched the flutter of her heavy-lidded eyes and the curl of a contented smile on her lips.

Lying back against her bed with her slender body curled up on top of his was the stuff fantasies were made of. He ran his hand down her back, over her pert buttocks, and allowed his fingertips to skim the tops of her knee-highs. *So hot... She was like a naughty schoolgirl.*

The whole thing had escalated so quickly. He'd had no intention of taking her to bed when he'd offered her a ride home. He'd been noble in his desire to make sure she was safe. But seeing her open up had flicked some kind of switch. She was so incredibly beautiful when she was vulnerable—something he suspected she hated to be.

He'd wanted nothing more than to make her pain go away. Still, part of him worried that he'd taken advantage of her weakness.

She shifted on top of him, rubbing against his lower body and causing him to stir. Hell, they'd barely finished and he was ready to go again. It had been a long time since he'd had sex sober, let alone with someone who wasn't a random football groupie. She was different in every possible way from what he was used to, and he'd enjoyed it far more than he wanted to. He wasn't supposed to feel this way.

He buried his face against her neck to block out the confusing thoughts.

'Once not enough for you?' Jasmine asked, her voice low and gravelly in his ear. She circled her hips against him.

Groaning, he pressed up against her heat while his lips found hers. Her rosebud lips were pink and puffy, her taste delectable.

'I get the impression it would never be enough with you,' Grant said.

Her face hovered inches over him, her lips brushing his cheeks and nose. Grant looked up into her warm brown eyes and lost himself for a moment.

After sex he wanted to run, to put as much distance as possible between him and the woman he'd slept with. He needed to reclaim his space, his privacy. It happened every single time…except now. The usual twitching of his muscles and the restlessness in his hands seemed far away. His eyes weren't roaming the room; his mind wasn't formulating an exit strategy. He'd never needed to specify a 'one night only' rule before—it was his MO—but the whole concept seemed ridiculous with Jasmine. There was no way one night would be enough.

Now he wanted to revel in the feeling of her. It scared the hell out of him. A sigh escaped him as her thighs pressed up against his sides and he watched the way her thick lashes touched each time she blinked. Through the twinges of guilt he was hyperaware of her presence, as though he could notice every miniscule movement. Every breath, every strand of hair as it fell about her.

'I'm guessing this is a first,' he said, gripping her slim waist and shifting so they lay side by side. He brought his lips down to her neck and she muttered her enjoyment. 'Considering I'm a student and all.'

'You're the only legal male I teach.' Her lips gave a small teasing smile. 'So, yes. Though it's…it's been a while for me.'

'Me too.'

He wasn't sure why she'd told him that, and he was even less sure of why he'd responded. Part of proving himself to be the reformed and focused athlete he was had meant giving up the partying…and that had meant giving up the girls—at least for the most part. Staying away from relationships had been easy; he didn't need to be burned twice. But staying away from physical intimacy had been difficult when at first he'd wanted to fill the void of loneliness with something. But being with Jasmine was so much more than scratching an itch.

Part of him wanted to talk to her—to divulge all his troubles and faults, to strip himself bare. But it couldn't happen. Besides, they'd made a pact.

'Two peas.'

She looked at him, her eyes shining. But there was something tentative about the way she touched him, something careful in her movements, and that told him she was as unsure as he was.

He pressed his lips together for fear that he might spill out more than he wanted to. There was something powerful about Jasmine—something that made him feel he might finally be able to open up.

Thoughts like that were both dangerous and stupid. He'd done enough damage to his life without baring his sins to someone he had no reason to trust. For an AFL player, or anyone in the limelight, that was practically asking for a front-page news headline: Secret Lover Tells All. And unfortunately there was no statute of limitations on sports gossip. He'd borne the brunt of that before, and he was never going back there again.

Hooking her leg around his, she wrapped her foot around his calf and shimmied closer. The soft touch of her fingertips slid over his chest and down towards his stomach. Closing his eyes, he pushed the worry from his mind. Now was a time for pleasure—pure and unadulterated pleasure. As her hand dipped lower it became easier for him to focus on the steady path she drew around his bellybutton towards his growing erection.

'I think you've taught me a thing or two already.' Grant brought his hands up to her hair, pushing his fingers through the thick glossy strands until he cupped the curve of her head. 'I'm sure those *plié* things will come in handy at some point.'

'You'll be thanking me when your Achilles' tendons are strong and flexible.'

'Flexibility is certainly a plus.' He struggled to get the words out as Jasmine pressed against him.

'It *does* come in handy.'

His body lurched with the image of Jasmine bent in two and he growled in appreciation. 'I know this is a one-time thing, but I don't think once will do it justice.'

'It's like you read my mind…'

He pulled her beneath him, leaning down to kiss a trail

from the gentle sweep of her small breasts to her stomach. He couldn't help but smile as she giggled when his lips brushed over her most ticklish parts. He continued down to the smooth skin of her sex, his senses sparking at the sharp intake of breath when he pressed his lips gently to the most private part of her. She tasted sweet and feminine and carnal.

Her body opened to his touch, porcelain thighs falling apart and welcoming him. Her hands found their way to his head, fingers tangling in his hair as she gripped him. He traced the line of her with his tongue, enjoying the way she arched to his mouth with such wanton need. She was slick with desire, her body primed for him.

He found the sensitive bud of her clitoris and concentrated his energy there. Her hands were curled into the fabric of the bedspread as she bucked against him, seeking the release he held out of reach. When he paused momentarily she cried out.

'Don't stop…' Her voice was strangled. 'Please.'

'I've only got one night, remember?' He rested his chin on her lower belly. 'Don't rush me.'

He ran his hands up and down her legs, toying with the edges of her knee-highs. He hooked his fingers underneath the elastic and went to peel one from her.

She gasped. 'No!'

'It's OK,' he soothed, his voice low and quiet, as though he were convincing a frightened animal not to run from him.

'No.'

She shook her head, and the tremble of her lip almost undid him. She was far from the writhing, sensual beauty of a minute ago. Her pale face and sad eyes sliced away at his composure. He remembered the shame in her eyes as she'd talked about her accident, the self-loathing he understood with a painful acuity.

'Let me see you,' he said, reaching up to clasp her hands. Her delicate wrists were fragile in his grip, trembling beneath his fingertips. 'Please.'

'It's ugly.' She squeezed her eyes shut, her head angled away from him.

'Jasmine, open your eyes.' He was firm, determined to be strong for her. 'Open them for me.'

She did as he asked, her eyes shimmering beneath heavy lashes. She let out a shaky breath as he brought his hands back down to her calves.

'You're stunning.' His voice was rough, emotional. 'Scars or no scars.'

She gave a slight nod of her head, the most minimal of movements, but he wasn't going to proceed until he got her consent. His lips pressed against her knee and followed the line of her shin as he peeled her sock away from the skin. The room was heavy with silence; she was holding her breath so that all that could be heard was the thundering of his heart. The ankle she'd injured recently had yellow patches discolouring the skin. The swelling had gone down, but the marks on her skin would remain awhile longer.

He moved to the other sock and revealed the leg injured in her accident. The scar was bright red against her fair skin; it snaked up the side of her leg and finished a few inches under her knee. He looked up and saw that she had her eyes clamped shut again, her bottom lip between her teeth. His heart burst at her fear.

'I tried to warn you.' Her voice quivered.

Grant pushed up from his position on the bed; locking his eyes on hers. 'I don't care that you have scars.'

His fingertips gently traced the length of her injured leg. He treated it as though it were as precious and beautiful as the rest of her...because it was. He pressed himself against her, pushing her body into the soft depths of the bed.

'We all have scars…even if you can't see anything on the outside.' His lips trailed the length of her jaw until he reached her ear. 'If you think even for a second that I'm bothered, then I'll stop right now.'

She stared up at him, uncertainty flickering across her face. Each second felt like hours as Grant held himself there, waiting for her to call the next move.

'Don't stop.' Her voice was the barest whisper.

He brought his hands to the insides of her thighs and lowered himself down her body. He ran his tongue up the delicate join of her hip, working his way back to her centre. A moan—soft and delicate—urged him on.

Something within him shattered as her eyes fluttered shut. She pressed another condom into his hand and he sheathed himself before entering her with a single, smooth thrust. Jasmine clenched instinctively around him, her body responding to his as though they were made for each other.

The tension had melted from her face and her wide eyes glimmered up at him. Her full lips were parted, a pink flush warming her cheeks. She was stunning.

She lifted her hips so that he could hook his arms underneath her thighs and drive deeper into her. Each thrust sent pleasure shooting through him. His entire body was alight with the feeling of her. She lifted her legs higher, draping her ankles over his shoulders, and giggled at the delight on his face.

'Being a dancer does have its perks.' She smiled up at him, the confidence blossoming on her face once more.

'No kidding.' He ran his hands up and down her legs, taking care to be gentle over her scars but not wanting to leave any part of her out of his worship. 'Your body is amazing—every goddamn inch of it.'

His careful strokes were aimed at putting pressure in the spot where she needed it most; she clenched around him as her pleasure mounted. It was all he could do to control himself, to stop himself from ravishing her.

'I need it now…' Jasmine tipped her head back, exposing the delicate white skin of her neck. Grant kissed her there, she shivered and a soft moan escaped her lips.

He moved harder and faster, pushing her towards release with each thrust, until her fingers dug into his back, her nails scratching at his skin as she peaked. The sound of her crying out his name brought him to a sudden and powerful climax.

Exhausted, he fell forwards. His face was cradled in the sweet curve of her neck, where she smelled of pleasure and satisfaction and wonder. The room was silent as they clung to one another as if their lives depended on it.

CHAPTER TEN

GRANT HAD BEEN tempted to slip out of Jasmine's apartment when the sky had not yet encountered the pink whisper of dawn. After they'd ravaged one another for a second time Jasmine had fallen asleep curled into his side, her French knickers hanging from the post at the end of the bed.

The temptation of her lithe body tucked into his had been far too much. The way she slept—with her hair fanned out over the pillow and a small smile on her lips—had made Grant want to stare at her until the image was permanently embedded in his mind. He'd known he should get out before she decided to wake and go for round number three...as good as that sounded.

But he hadn't been able to bring himself to do it. Thinking about leaving her had caused his heart to clench. What would she make of a silent departure?

She said herself it was a one-time thing. Though his logic was faultless, he couldn't help but worry that she might conclude that he viewed her as a one-night stand—nothing more.

So he'd stayed, savouring her body against his. His mind swirled with confusion. This girl was going to bring him undone.

One slender arm draped over his midsection. Her nails were painted baby pink and in the pale morning light they shimmered like pearls. Everything about her was graceful and dainty, yet she'd turned out to be a tightly wound bundle of sexual heat.

His coach's voice echoed in his head: *Don't replace one crutch with another.* He had to make sure that this thing with Jasmine—whatever it was—remained casual. He couldn't afford to fall into anything serious...not while his reputation was hanging in the balance. He needed a big win this season to get his career back on track.

Even as he warned himself he ached at the thought of leaving her. He was in trouble...big trouble.

Jasmine shifted, her sleepy movement causing her small naked breasts to rub against him. He felt himself stiffen beneath the cotton bedsheet and he had to contain the guttural groan that threatened to burst forth. She had the most *incredible* effect on him.

Her eyes fluttered open, dark lashes blinking as a shy smile spread across her lips. 'Well, that escalated, didn't it?'

Grant chuckled and pulled Jasmine closer to him. Her hair swept over her, the glossy lengths giving her a goddesslike appearance. He ran his hands through the gleaming strands, enjoying the silken sensation against his palms.

'No regrets?' He searched her face.

'We didn't do anything to regret.' Her face was buried into his side, her lashes tickling his ribcage as she blinked.

'You should be able to look me in the eye, then.'

She peered up, her cheeks pink. 'No regrets. I promise.'

Silence settled over them until all that could be heard were the sounds of normal life occurring outside. Inside, life was anything but normal. They'd crossed a line that could not be uncrossed, no matter how they tried to rationalise it away.

Jasmine rolled onto her back, eyes locked onto the ceiling. 'So...'

'So?'

They looked at one another and laughed. 'This is…'

'It's only awkward if we let it be awkward.' He rolled onto his side to face her. 'I know our one night is over, but I propose coffee.'

Her eyes lit up at the suggestion of coffee—it was like a moment of pure sunshine. 'I never say no to coffee.'

She hadn't been sure of how Grant would react the morning after, though part of her was relieved he hadn't made some lame excuse to run away. Or, worse still, made a sneaky exit in the middle of the night. Her fragile self-esteem wouldn't have been able to take it. However, what it now meant was that they were standing awkwardly in her kitchen, making small talk.

In some ways that was worse than nursing a bruised ego. She should never have gone down this path in the first place. You didn't have to force conversation with a fantasy—nor did you have to make it a cappuccino.

She folded her arms across her chest, pulling her baggy sweater closer around her. Her feet were bare, and the cold of the tiles seeped into her bones. She'd thrown on a pair of leggings to cover up her scars—not that it made much difference at this point.

How had she allowed him to see so much of her last night? Was she that desperate for affection that she let him take over? He'd been tender beyond what she'd expected, his gentle handling of her more visible flaws better than she could have hoped for. But the dark part of her mind—the blackened recess where Kyle had once burried his claws—told her that he was secretly disgusted.

How could he not be?

She turned to the coffee machine, hoping he couldn't hear the shame that roared within her at full force. She let out a breath, forcing herself to be silent as the machine whirred to life. She twisted the too-long sleeves of her jumper, covering her hands completely as though it might protect her.

'About last night—' he started.

'If you say *How was it for you?* I'm going to brain you with this mug.' She waved a coffee mug at him as if to illustrate her point.

'What?' A sly smile spread over his lips as he leant against the breakfast bar. 'You got a problem with giving positive reinforcement?'

She poked her tongue out at him.

'No matter—I'll take the fact that you screamed the house down to mean I did a good job.'

'Do you want this coffee or not?' Her cheeks flamed, but she couldn't prevent a smile twitching at her lips. He was cocky, but then again, when you were that good....

She held his cup under the coffee machine and filled it with steaming dark liquid. The scent filled the room. Usually it was the most comforting scent in the world— reminiscent of early-morning ballet rehearsals and catch-ups with Elise—but today it did nothing to quell her morning-after jitters. Weren't people supposed to feel anxious *before* sex, not after?

'I've heard of love 'em and leave 'em, but never love 'em and cease all conversation,' he teased.

'We don't need to cease *all* conversations.'

'Just ones pertaining to sex?'

'Yes.' She filled her own mug and brought it close to her face. Inhaling deep, she willed the curling tendrils of steam to work their magic, but her shoulders remained bunched, her hands in a death-grip around the mug's handle.

'So...how about that local sports team?' He drummed his fingers against the countertop.

'That would be you.'

'Right.' Grant took a sip of his coffee and paused for a moment. 'Why don't you like talking about sex?'

'Don't pull your psychology voodoo on me.' Getting psychoanalysed was the *last* thing she needed right now. She was having a hard time dealing with her own thoughts without someone else picking them apart.

'I'm only asking—'

'Sex is for doing, not for talking about.'

'Only if you're repressed,' he muttered.

'Based on what you saw last night, do you think I'm repressed?' she asked, but as he opened his mouth to answer she cut him off. 'It's a rhetorical question. I don't see why we need to make a big deal out of it. It was one night between two consenting adults...who never need to speak about it again.'

'Point taken,' he said.

Jasmine experienced a strange twinge of emptiness when Grant left, though she had no right whatsoever to feel that way. After all, she was the one who'd enforced the 'one night only' rule and made it clear commitment wasn't on the agenda. She tried to focus on other things as soon as the door closed behind him, and knew she was in trouble when she waited by the door until the sound of his car vanished down the street. Yeah, she was in trouble, all right.

So it turned out that Grant Farley wasn't just an ace football player, but he also had some other—more carnal—skills at his disposal. He'd rocked her world in a way that had surprised her, and she couldn't help reliving the night in her head.

Over and over and *over*.

'Earth to Jasmine.' Elise waved a hand in front of her face. 'Anyone home?'

'Huh?' Jasmine shook her head and focused on her friend. 'Sorry, I drifted off then.'

'I'll say.' Elise eyed her suspiciously. 'And judging by

the expression on your face I'd say you drifted somewhere muscular.'

Jasmine gave Elise a light punch in the arm, but the smile that refused to leave her lips revealed enough. Elise's eyes widened until they looked as though they might pop right out of her pretty little head.

'You *didn't*?' She grabbed Jasmine's face and examined it. Jasmine twisted away, but Elise was stronger than her petite frame would suggest. 'You *did!*'

'Fine.' Jasmine batted her friend away. 'Twice, if you must know.'

Elise's mouth opened and closed in shock. Eventually she let out a surprised laugh.

'The goldfish look isn't good on you,' Jasmine said, rolling her eyes.

'I'm just surprised.' Elise picked up a costume from the bag on the table and commenced sewing a row of sequins. 'I'm guessing it went well, otherwise you wouldn't be grinning like a court jester...'

'It did go well.' Jasmine sewed a matching costume, her hands practised in the simple up and down threading motion. 'In fact I could say I haven't experienced anything that good in a long time. If ever.'

Jasmine had forgotten all about her promise to assist Elise with the costumes for an upcoming dance competition. When Elise had arrived with enough sequins to make a small nation sparkle Jasmine had had no choice but to hope that she didn't look as loved up and dishevelled as she felt.

'I guess football players have a lot of practice.' Elise propped her chin in one hand, her face alight.

'He was...' Jasmine paused, thinking of the best way to describe him. 'I don't know...more tender than I expected. More considerate.'

Elise raised an eyebrow.

'Don't get me wrong, it was still hot as hell, but he wasn't as self-focused as I expected. He seemed to get a kick out of pleasuring me.'

'Good.' Elise nodded her approval and went back to her sewing. 'I won't stand for you dating any more selfish bastards—you've had your share.'

Jasmine nodded. Though her dating experience was minimal, she did seem to have a type—heartless bastards with more money than feelings. If it had only been Kyle she could have chalked it up to bad luck. One was a mistake; three was a trend.

She yawned. A night of passionate lovemaking might have been good for the soul, but it wasn't great for her energy levels. She was in desperate need of another coffee and a blanket.

'So how did you go?' Elise abandoned her sewing and went to the coffee machine, as if reading Jasmine's mind. 'With the whole leg…thing…'

'That wasn't easy. I tried to keep my socks on, but he wasn't having a bar of that.'

'You tried to keep your socks on while you were having sex?' Elise seemed unsure of whether Jasmine was joking or not, and her delicate features pulled into a frown. 'You're not an old married couple.'

'It wasn't like that—they were knee-highs and it was kind of sexy…a bit of a naughty schoolgirl thing.'

'Well, that's OK.' She came back to the table with two coffees. 'But still…*socks?*'

Jasmine laughed, her mind wandering back to the way he'd peeled those socks from her. It had been the single most petrifying thing she'd ever experienced. Give her a packed house at State Theatre over that any day of the week.

Damn him for leaving her so unsettled. The whole idea of sleeping with him had been to get it out of her system.

But she was thinking about him more than ever. Damn, damn, *damn*.

'Have you looked him up on the internet yet?' Elise's eyes lit up. She had on her scary I've-got-a-wild-and-crazy-plan face. Jasmine had seen that face before.

It never ended well.

'No,' she replied, drawing the sound out slowly. She wasn't the most tech-savvy of people, and the internet stalking habits of her generation confused her. What was wrong with a little mystery?

'Oh, this is happening!' Elise jumped up from her seat, snatched her coffee from the table and made a break for the study.

'Dear God...' Jasmine started after her, her limp preventing speedy mobility.

The study—which was more of a glorified broom closet than a legitimate working room—was already alive with the sounds of Elise's hands flying across the keyboard. She typed like a woman possessed.

Elise jumped out of the desk chair, allowing Jasmine to sit, but retained control of the mouse. The search engine spat out a seemingly endless amount of 'Grant Farley' links. The images that popped up showed shots of Grant in action on the football pitch, as well as a younger Grant with a bounty of beautiful girls on his arm—she recognised two of them as Australian models on the rise.

Seeing photos of famous men and their trophy women made her stomach churn. It was a little too close to home.

'Did you see that?' Elise leaned in, clicking on one of the photos.

Red carpet shots from the previous year's Brownlow Medal sent shivers down Jasmine's spine. The man certainly scrubbed up well in a suit. One blonde woman came up with him repeatedly—captions identified her as Chelsea Aims, fiancée of Grant Farley.

Jasmine raised an eyebrow. This was the first she'd heard of him having a fiancée. Looking more closely at the pictures, she could see the photos featuring Chelsea were old. Grant's face showed the youthful glow of a young man in his prime. He lacked the serious, square-jawed look he now wore permanently, and he seemed lighter...happier.

When the photos of Chelsea stopped there were a few of Grant suited up with a brooding stare—much closer to the way he looked today—standing alone on the red carpet.

Elise flicked over the articles section of the search engine. There was a link to the official Jaguars website, and a few articles referencing him when the Jaguars merger had taken place. But one headline stood out in particular: Jaguars Star Grant Farley Falls from Grace.

'Oooh, what's this?' Elise clicked on the link and both girls waited with bated breath.

As a picture of a very bleary-eyed Grant appeared on the screen, Jasmine sucked in a breath. Holding his hand up in an attempt to cover his face, though doing a poor job of it, Grant appeared to be stumbling, and there was a smear of something red across his fitted white T-shirt.

Farther down there was another picture of him, looking very sombre, wearing a dark suit and an open-necked shirt. The caption read: 'Grant Farley leaves court in Melbourne after pleading not guilty to assault charges.'

The article detailed the incident: a bar fight that had ended up with two men being hospitalised. It mentioned that the assault charges had been dropped after the matter had been settled out of court, which could only be code for using his money to make his problems go away.

'That doesn't sound like him at all.'

Jasmine couldn't keep the quiver out of her voice. The article showed a person very different from the tender, passionate man she'd come to know. Sure, he was a typical football player—headstrong and iron-willed—but she couldn't imagine him beating two men to a pulp and then paying them off.

It didn't sound right. Yet she couldn't deny the heaviness that settled in the pit of her stomach like lead. Perhaps it was a good thing they had decided on a one-night-only rule. She'd already been with a man who thought he could buy his way out of anything, and he'd ended up treating her like another investment.

With the end of the football season looming, Grant was more focused than ever. This was his opportunity to put the past behind him. He'd cleaned himself up, kept off the partying and was playing the best footy of his life. As much as he hated to admit it, the ballet was doing him a world of good…and not only due to the magical touch of one very sexy ballet teacher.

The weeks since he'd slept with Jasmine had gone by in a blur. He'd missed a few lessons as the preparation for footy finals increased. It was the last week of August and they were only a month out from Grand Final. The Jaguars had been hovering around the top of the ladder for the last three rounds—not a first in the club's history but certainly a first in the past few years.

He wanted to be a part of them making the Grand Final for the first time in the past decade, and he knew it was his moment to show the team and the fans that he was a changed man. That he'd moved on from his mistakes and that he could be the player they all wanted him to be. He was so close he could taste it.

Jasmine had been distracted too. She seemed absent during their lessons but he assumed she was as focused on recovering from her injury and other ballet stuff as he was on his footy. Though it hadn't stopped him thinking about revisiting their fantasy-provoking scorcher of a night together.

Today he watched as she wrapped up her lesson with some of her older students, her beautiful face pulled into the look of concentration he now knew well. She clapped her hands together and gave a pep talk to the group.

'Well done, ladies,' he said as he entered the studio, passing the students on their way out.

One winked at him and the other women tittered amongst themselves, blushing under his praise. At one point he would have enjoyed the blatant adoration, but now his tastes seemed to run more to the snarky sting of a former ballerina with a soft, sensual centre.

'Your effect on women is sickening,' Jasmine drawled, standing with her hands on her hips.

That's more like it. His heart kicked up a notch and his lips were unable to resist a smile.

'I don't do it on purpose,' he replied, leaning against the *barre* and cocking his head to one side.

She rolled her eyes. 'Tell me you don't love it. You relish the sex-symbol status.'

Ha! She made it sound as if he was one of those vain sportsmen who supplemented their incomes by modelling jocks or something ridiculous like that. He'd even turned down a spot in a Most Eligible Bachelor competition because he hated all the attention. These days if people were paying attention to him he wanted it to be because of his footy. Nothing else.

'I'm a country boy.' He thrust a hand through his hair, his fingers pushing the strands away from his face. 'I *don't* see myself as a sex symbol.'

The words sounded weird coming from his mouth—unnatural. In his experience girls were after more than looks. What mattered were important three-letter acronyms like VIP and MVP, and *lots* of zeros on your bank statement. Looks were a bonus.

'But you are,' she replied, her tone cool. 'A quick internet search will tell you that.'

'Have you been stalking me?' He laughed. The thought of her poring over images of him online seemed ridiculous.

Never mind the fact that he'd done *exactly* the same thing. He'd trawled through photos of her dancing *en pointe* and even found a video of one of her Australian Ballet performances and watched it, enraptured.

'It's not stalking if you're looking up someone famous.'

His heart stilled. What had she been looking for? A mask of calm slipped over his face. As he'd said to her before, fame was an unfortunate by-product of his career. A necessary evil. Something he put up with because it was part of the deal.

In truth, after the paparazzi hell he'd endured as part of the court proceedings he'd be happy never to see another camera again. But life didn't work that way, and sometimes you had to slap a smile on your face even when you wanted to drop an F-bomb. Swallowing, he forced himself to relax. This was Jasmine, not some fame-hungry groupie.

'You *know* I'd prefer to play footy without the added extras.' He walked over to the *barre* and got himself ready for their warm-up. 'Although there are some perks to the celebrity aspect.'

'Like what?'

'Like the fact that I get to take dates along to fancy functions,' he said, keeping his tone even. 'You should come along to one.'

He hadn't planned on using the invitation as a test to see what her intentions were, but when she'd said she'd been looking him up online a funny feeling had settled in his stomach. He wanted so desperately for her to be the woman he'd come to know—for her to be so very different from all the women he'd been with before.

'Excuse me?' Her eyes widened.

'The Brownlow is coming up.' He leant forwards, watching her intently. 'I want you to come with me.'

Jasmine stood there, her mouth agape. He'd gone stag in the past, but it had usually ended up with the other WAGs pairing him with one of their friends/sisters/cousins. They were seldom good company and *always* in it for the chance to get their picture in the papers. Taking Jasmine would mean having a shield against those annoying matchmaking offers, *and* he'd have the pleasure of seeing her dressed up to the nines. Something told him that she'd outshine every other woman there by a mile.

Yeah, he wanted this firecracker with her smart mouth and gorgeous smile by his side all night. He could only hope that she'd want to be by his side for the person he was—not for the other reasons people usually gravitated towards him.

'I don't think so.' She shook her head, her dark brows pulling together. 'I'm not the red-carpet type.'

He stepped forwards, closing the space between them. 'It's all very glamorous.'

Mixed emotions churned in his gut. On one hand the fact that she hadn't jumped at the invitation meant she wasn't after the limelight. On the other hand he hadn't expected her to decline his invitation flat-out.

Wasn't it every girl's dream to frock up and walk down a red carpet? He'd even called in a favour with an old acquaintance who was a designer. The gown was wrapped up in a huge box hidden in his linen closet with a note he'd written himself. *That* was a first—notes and cards and gifts were way out of his MO.

Usually the girl would ask for something before he'd even had the chance to offer. Perhaps Jasmine *was* perfect for him. He frowned to himself.

'Why don't you take someone from your family?'

Her voice brought him back to the present.

'I want *you*.'

She drew her lower lip between her teeth. She could block him out with a lowering of her thick dark lashes if she liked, but he'd seen the heat that flared bright and brilliant. He'd seen the black of her pupils expand at his words *I want you*.

'Jasmine, I could take anyone. I bet if I asked any of the teachers from this ballet school they would come with me at the drop of a hat—Elise included.'

She frowned. 'Your point?'

'I don't want anyone else.' He brushed his hand down the length of her arm, sucking in a breath at the way goosebumps rippled along her skin at his touch. 'I want you to come with me. I plan to win, and when I do I want you to help me celebrate. Think about it.'

'Fine.' She smiled stiffly, the curve of her lips a mismatch with the guarded expression in her eyes.

She crossed her arms on her chest, guarding herself. Something was amiss. What was going on with Jasmine Bell?

CHAPTER ELEVEN

JASMINE WAS STUNNED, he'd asked her—no, *told* her—she should be his date to the Brownlow. This wasn't in line with their one-night-only rule, and frankly the idea of having cameras shoved in her face while they posed on the red carpet turned her stomach. The Brownlow was the biggest off-field football event of the year, and even as a complete sports dunce she was well aware of the event's prestige.

Did he want her as arm candy? She'd been there, done that. Having Kyle parade her around like a piece of designer luggage had been bad enough, but at least back then there had been something in it for her—a chance to further her career. Now Grant wanted her to do the same thing. Why? Surely he had his pick of the pretty young things who normally attended those events. They were the type of girls who craved attention, with their hair extensions and fake tans, the ones happy to have their photo taken.

Girls *not* like her.

There was no way she'd accept his offer. She'd figure out a way to let him down gently, and until then she'd keep it one hundred per cent professional between them. There had been a tiny part of her that had entertained the idea of seeing Grant again, but his world was too different from hers. It had all the hallmarks of what she'd hated about her former life.

They stood at the *barre,* their bodies close as they

worked through the warm-up. Jasmine had been keeping her distance from Grant, yet every time she was near him her body rebelled. The tips of her fingers tingled with the need to touch, to explore. Her blood pulsed harder when he was around, and her heart fluttered at the mere signal of his presence.

But she knew it was the wrong path for her. She'd promised herself when she left the Australian Ballet that her days of being someone else's puppet were over. She wasn't sure what it was that incited men to try to control her, tell her what to do. That was why it was easier to stay away.

Then she could speak for herself. She could be her own person. Unfortunately it also meant she couldn't be a part of Grant's world.

'I read an interesting article about you,' she said.

'There's a lot of stuff on the internet.' He shrugged.

She could tell that beneath the blasé gesture he was hiding his true emotions and immediately jumping on the defensive. The relaxed stance didn't match the hard set of his jaw, nor the acute focus of his light blue eyes.

'Was it anything of particular interest?' he asked.

She paused for a second. Why was she even bringing this up? She knew that the majority of news relating to famous people was pure fiction. Did she believe that Grant was the person the gossip site had made him out to be?

No, she didn't believe it. But something deep within her compelled her to find out the truth. She *had* to know. Perhaps if she had another reason to push him away she'd be able to keep her distance. Lord knew she needed help in that department.

'The one about you paying off those guys you got in a fight with.' She knew the moment she saw him stiffen that she'd hit a sore spot.

'Excuse me?'

'I saw the pictures of you leaving court...'

Fire blazed in his eyes and she thought for a moment that he might scream at her. But his voice came out deadly calm.

'And?'

'I want to know your side of the story.'

He raked a hand through his hair and stared through her. He had asked so many questions of her, pressed her about her dancing. Didn't she deserve to know him too?

The studio was so silent she could hear the cars driving on the rain-slicked road outside.

'Why?'

'Do I need a reason? I don't believe the things they said—'

'I paid them off.' The words were sharper than a blade. 'I did it.'

She shook her head. 'There's more to it than that.'

'How would you know?' He seemed to sneer at her, his features fixed into a frightening mask of calm.

'Because I know you, Grant. You're not like that.'

His Adam's apple bobbed in his throat as he choked the words out. 'I did it.'

'You hit them?'

'No.' The mask was slipping, cracks showing through to the vulnerability he'd no doubt become accustomed to hiding. 'I was too drunk out of my mind to even get past the first swing in that fight.'

'I knew it.'

'But I did pay them.'

'Why did you pay them if you didn't hit them?' She shook her head. 'That doesn't make sense.'

'Because the club wanted it to go away as quickly as possible. We couldn't take the bad press —not when we'd struggled through the past few years. We were losing sponsors...'

Jasmine's stomach pitched from side to side.

He continued. 'They'd rather let me appear to be the guilty party than risk damage to the club. There's a good chance I would have been cleared, based on the witness accounts and footage from the pub security cameras, but they didn't want to risk the media crawling all over us during the court case if it dragged on.'

He glowered at her, his mouth pulled tight into a line. Had she pushed too far? No, she deserved to know. They were friends...sort of.

'I'm not perfect—far from it. But I'm not violent.'

'I know.'

'Then why did you ask?' His expression softened, the defences slipping from him as his body relaxed.

'I wanted to hear the truth. I wanted to...get to know you.' She bit down on her lip, confused by the emotions running around in her.

'You *do* know me.' He uncrossed his arms.

'Not really,' she said. 'I know *about* you, but you seem to do all the asking when we're together. I feel like you know me but I don't know you. I wanted to know the real you.'

'Fame is hard work,' he said with a sad smile. 'It makes you wary of anyone asking questions. I guess I've become a little more defensive than I realised.'

'I can understand that.'

'I imagine it's the same with ballet,' he said, taking a step towards her. 'Didn't you want to dance and forget about everything else?'

'Yeah.' She nodded.

Her whole body tingled with awareness as he closed the gap between them. On their first ballet lesson she'd seen a beef-head football player who thought he was a god. Now she saw a complex, intelligent, misunderstood man. No god, just a man.

'I was a simple kid from the country who loved playing footy.'

'You were dazzled by the big smoke?'

'Damn straight.' He reached for her, his large hand wrapping around her smaller one. 'I was dazzled by all the beautiful girls.'

'You're full of it,' she whispered.

Energy crackled between them. The rest of the world fell away as he pulled her to him.

'I left my family behind. I left a quiet, dull life full of expectation and burden. Everything here was exciting and I was like a kid in a candy store.'

'And you ate too much candy.' She could feel it. The ease with which he'd been swept up by his success was believable and forgivable.

'I gorged myself on it until I was sick.' He brought his lips down to hers, cupping her face in his hands. 'And speaking of things I want to gorge myself on...'

She blew out a breath, knowing exactly where he was going. What she didn't know was if she could stop it.

'Are you reconsidering your one-night rule?' Grant asked, nuzzling her neck. 'You're looking at me like I'm dinner.'

'You're quite sure of yourself, aren't you?' Jasmine tilted her chin up at him, studying his features. There was something utterly disarming about him. The combination of his strong jaw and the slightly crooked, freckle-smattered nose enchanted her.

His voice was low, predatory. 'I'm not asking you to stop.'

In one swift movement Grant had pulled Jasmine to him and pressed her up against the *barre,* his hands gripping the wooden rail on either side of her hips so that she was trapped. He pressed urgently against her, and she arched to him with equal candour. She ran her hands up the sides of his thighs, skimming the tight curve of his behind until her hands reached his back.

'You're getting there...' she said, her voice catching. With each second that passed Jasmine's resistance was falling harder.

'I want you to wrap those incredibly flexible legs around me so I can make you scream.' His eyes were hooded, his voice coarse with lust. 'Again.'

Before he could say anything else she pressed up against him, her mouth hungry for more. Grant's arms wrapped around her, encircling her waist as he lifted her up so that she could wrap herself around him. Grant carried her weight seemingly without effort as she pressed against him, her breasts hard against his chest.

'Not here,' she whispered.

Jasmine fidgeted in the car, her hands unwilling to be still as Grant drove them back to his apartment. She was out of control. The fearful voice inside her told her she was crazy. She didn't *do* reckless, and this was pretty damn reckless.

There were rules and boundaries that she needed to adhere to. Jasmine liked those things. There was a reason she loved ballet enough to make it her life. Ballet was all about rules, about precision. These things made her comfortable. But this...this was something else entirely.

Her 'one night only' was turning into a spontaneous night number two, and she was powerless to stop it.

'Penny for your thoughts, Miss Bell?' Grant's voice was teasing, and he watched her as he held the car straight along the freeway.

'Not a penny's worth.' She sank down lower in the comfy leather seat. 'I'm just admiring the view.'

The city was drawing closer. The ethereal orange glow that encompassed the tall buildings of Melbourne's CBD grew nearer with each minute. Jasmine loved the city. The lights had fascinated her as a child—she'd always wondered how something could exist for so long without ever sleeping.

'The view will get a lot better than this.' His eyes raked her slouched form. 'I promise.'

'Are you always so smooth with the ladies?' Jasmine propped herself up on one arm and watched him as he laughed, the sound rumbling deep within him. It curled her insides.

'Hardly.' His lips turned up into a sardonic smile. 'The sad fact is footy players don't need to be much of anything to have the girls lined up.'

Jasmine screwed up her nose at him. The thought of a gaggle of screaming girls surrounding Grant made her stomach churn. 'So you've become lazy?'

'I haven't become anything,' he said, frowning at her insinuation. 'Those girls aren't my style. I like 'em feisty… like you.'

'Flattery won't get you anywhere.' She gave his arm a playful shove.

'Correct me if I'm wrong, but I've already got somewhere.' His eyes glinted in the reflection of the streetlights. 'You are in my car, on your way to my apartment, are you not?'

'Details…' She waved her hand, dismissing his argument.

'Have you thought any more about the dancing thing?'

'No,' she lied. She'd been thinking about it constantly… or rather trying *not* to think about it constantly.

'I asked you to promise me that you wouldn't stop trying.'

'I remember you asking, but I don't remember making such a promise.'

Grant pulled the car into the parking lot and killed the engine. 'I'd give anything to see you back up on a stage.'

'Why?' She unbuckled her seatbelt and turned to him.

'Because you're magnificent.' He leant over and crushed his mouth to hers.

He tasted faintly of mint and the scent of him invaded her nostrils, making her dizzy with lust. If he kept kissing her like that she might promise him anything.

They walked hand in hand to the building entrance and Jasmine marvelled at how luxurious it was inside. Her attention was diverted from him momentarily as they stepped into the Art Deco elevator, but he didn't give her long to marvel at the stylish design before he pulled her to him.

As the reflection of their embrace filled the ornate floor-to-ceiling mirrors she rested her body against the hard wall of his chest, enjoying the way he immediately curled his arms around her. His hands rested against her behind, pressing her against him so that she could feel his erection straining between them. She slipped her hand down to cup the bulge in his pants, enjoying the unrestrained groan that escaped his lips as she massaged him.

'Straight to business?'

'Yep.' She sucked at the curve of his neck. 'I find it stops you from asking questions.'

'Suits me fine.' He wound his hand through the length of her ponytail and gave a gentle tug, pulling her face up towards him. He landed a possessive kiss on her lips and she melted under him.

The elevator doors slid silently open. The hallway was empty. Tasteful watercolour paintings dotted the pale walls and grey carpet was soft underfoot. Their steps quickened with anticipation and heat shot through her arm where his hand wound tightly around hers, his fingers interlaced with her own.

Grant opened the door to his apartment and held it aside. She brushed past him, allowing her fingers to graze his hardness. A shiver ran down her spine; anticipation and excitement pooled in her belly.

The apartment was stark, a bachelor pad, with a large flat-screen TV as the focal point rather than the stunning view that filled the mammoth windows running the length of the room. The city lights dazzled against an inky winter sky and she lost her breath.

Grant took her hand again. 'It's better from the balcony.'

As he pushed open the sliding door the chilly air enveloped them. Jasmine stood against the railing, her hands gripping the bar tightly at her waist, and leaned over to look down on the city below. Noise from the remnants of city traffic, from people going about their evening and from the dinging of passing trams floated up to them. The scent of rain hung in the air. Grant stood behind her, pressing her against the protective balustrade, his lips on her neck.

'It's amazing,' she breathed, arching back against him. Her neck burned where he brushed his lips against the sensitive skin there. 'You're so lucky.'

'I am now.'

He squeezed, his hand trailing down her stomach until it brushed against the juncture of her thighs. She murmured as his hands slipped between her legs and stroked her heat. She was still in her leotard and tights with only a thick woollen coat to protect her from the cold. The thin fabric of the leotard provided little resistance to his hand, and she quivered as his fingers increased their pressure.

Turning around, Jasmine parted her legs so that Grant could press himself between them. She tilted her head back, enjoying the chilly rush of air across her face while her body burned beneath her coat. Feeling more than a little daring, she felt for his waistband and pulled down his pants, exposing his hardness to the night air.

She lapped up the surprise in Grant's eyes as she slid

down to a kneeling position in front of him and pressed her lips gently to the tip of him. He gripped the railing of the balustrade above her head.

Jasmine parted her lips and wrapped them around the head of his cock, sucking gently at first. He tasted salty. She brushed her tongue against his length, feeling him tremble against her. She slid him slowly out and then back in again, hearing him groan from above her as one hand clasped the back of her head.

'If you keep that up—' he warned, his voice strangled.

She drew back and looked up at him. His hand brushed her cheekbone as she stood in front of him. 'Then take me inside.'

They stumbled through the door into the living room and Grant tugged her along into his bedroom. A huge king-size bed dominated the room, covered in a simple navy bedspread that looked soft as a cloud.

There were no personal photos on the walls—nothing that gave away any clues about anyone in his life. She recalled him saying his relationship with his family was strained, but she hadn't expected to find an apartment devoid of *any* personal photos. The room was simply furnished and utilitarian. Only one picture hung on the wall—a large signed photograph of a football player that looked as though it might be from the seventies. She removed her coat and draped it over the back of a tub chair.

'Enough looking around.' Grant sat on the bed and drew her to him so that she was standing between his legs. He'd kicked off his pants and was sitting in his jumper. Reaching down, she pulled his jumper and T-shirt off with a single smooth movement.

'I'm looking at you now,' she whispered, climbing onto his lap so that she faced him with her legs straddling his waist.

Grant pulled down one of the straps on her leotard,

baring a small breast. His lips took in the sensitive bud of her nipple, causing a wave of pleasure to rush through her. Heat throbbed incessantly as his tongue flickered against her. A long drawn-out moan came out of her lips as her head lolled backwards.

He pulled on the other strap of her leotard and helped her arms out before he continued his attention to her breasts. Pushing away from him, Jasmine peeled off the leotard and let it drop to the floor around her ankles. Her tights and underwear followed, leaving a pool of nylon and cotton at her feet.

Grant ran his hands up the flat plane of Jasmine's stomach until they rested on her breasts. His fingers honed in on her erect nipples, rolling the rosy buds between his thumbs and forefingers, wringing a sharp cry of pleasure from her. Beneath his hands the worries of her world slipped away, her fears about her future, the pain of her loss...gone.

One hand came to dance over the smooth patch between her thighs, his fingers teasing apart the slick folds of flesh to find the tight bundle of nerves at her centre. Jasmine clenched tightly as his thumb found her and started its slow assault on her senses. She spasmed as waves of intense pleasure rolled over her until she reached breaking point. Orgasm shattered through her and light flared behind her shuttered eyes, her cries echoing off the walls of Grant's bedroom.

Spent, she collapsed against him and pressed a kiss to his cheek, feeling the roughness of his stubble against her tender lips. She felt safer than she had in a long time—as though the enclosure of his arms could protect her from the world.

CHAPTER TWELVE

SOME TIME LATER they lay tangled in the sheets of his bed, limbless with satisfaction and exhausted. Sex with Jasmine put to shame any of the workouts in his training regime. Grant took pride in the fact that she was limp and murmuring incoherent pleasure sounds against the crook of his neck. He'd be happy to listen to that sound for the rest of his life.

He rolled the thought around in his head. The rest of his life was a long time, considering he was generally fed up with someone after twenty-four hours. To go from a day to forever seemed…crazy. But the more time he spent with Jasmine the more he wanted. She'd become part of his life without him realising it, and going without her would be like going without air or food or any other life-giving necessity.

When had it happened?

'Grant?' His name was stretched out, half yawn, half groan. 'Am I dead?'

'Why do I feel like this is the start of a cheesy pick-up line?'

'It's a little too late for that, don't you think?' She laughed and stretched her legs out.

'Especially considering we broke the one-night-only rule,' he pointed out.

She traced her fingertip over his shoulder, outlining

the curves of his tattoo. 'That rule was put in place so no one got hurt. Therefore, if we don't hurt one another we should be OK.'

'Sounds good in theory.'

'And in practice?' She stilled beside him, her face tilted up.

'I'd like it to work in practice too.'

Like most things that sounded good in theory, reality was a little more complicated. But that didn't stop him wanting—for the first time in years—to see where reality could take them.

She reached up and pulled his face to her, kissing the corners of his lips, the tip of his nose. 'Sounds good to me.'

'So you'll come to the Brownlow with me, then?'

And just like that the post-sex glow was sucked out of the air. Jasmine's body tensed, her hand withdrawing from his face.

'I *said* I'd think about it.'

'What is there to think about?'

It figured that the one time he opened himself up he chose a woman who didn't want anything to do with his lifestyle. After a decade of people using him it was both a shock and a relief.

'Unless that's your way of stalling before you say no?' he added.

She sighed. 'I can't come to the Brownlow with you.'

'Why?'

'Do I need a reason?' She sat up on the bed and turned away from him.

'Call me curious.'

'I don't do the whole gala thing.' She raked her hands through her hair, twisting it and feeling around on the bed until she located her hair tie. 'I had to put up with it when I was with the Australian Ballet. Now I have a choice I choose *not* go to those things.'

'Sounds like there's some history behind that.'

'This is not a couch and I'm *not* your patient.' She tied her hair up and turned back to him, crossing her legs under her. 'You're a frustrated psychologist.'

'I'm observant,' he corrected. 'Not that I need to be...'

'Excuse me?'

'Anyone would be able to read you, Jasmine.'

'What's that supposed to mean?'

'You're an open book.' He reached out to place a hand on her knee. 'You might think you're good at hiding your emotions, but you're not.'

She pursed her lips. 'And?'

'I would rather have you on my arm than any of those other girls.' He sighed. 'You're not like them. That's what I like about you.'

'Really?' Her face softened and she traced the back of his hand with one delicate fingertip.

The sensation sent a ripple of awareness through him, though how his body could stir to life after what they'd done tonight was a complete mystery.

'I've been with those women before. I was engaged to one of them before she decided that I wasn't high enough up the food chain.' He swallowed the memories. That had been a long time ago and he was a different person now. 'I drank and partied myself into a hole, and I've been clawing my way out for twelve months. Something in my gut told me you were different.'

'I *am* different.' She lowered her eyes to her hands, wrapped into a neat ball in her lap. 'I'm *too* different—that's the problem.'

'That's crazy.'

'Is it? You said yourself I was nothing like the girls on the scene.' She paused. 'A life in the spotlight isn't what I want. My ex loved it—he dragged me to party after party so he could show me off. But that's all he wanted. It was never about me.'

'He was an idiot.'

'Yeah, he was.' She traced her fingertip over the pattern on the bed. 'But it put me off that kind of life. I don't want the whole world scrutinising me. I promised myself I wouldn't put myself in that position again. You understand that's why this can't be anything more than casual?'

Her face implored him and he wanted nothing more than to hold her until the past melted away. His chest ached. Could he offer her a life without public scrutiny? It seemed impossible, but something deep inside told him not to let her go. Maybe he could find a way to make it work. If he could keep her close until he built up enough trust, maybe then he could show her that he was different too. That he didn't want to show her off like some possession.

Even thinking the word made his blood boil. What he felt for Jasmine had nothing to do with possession. It was deeper than that. It was basic, fundamental.

'Fine.' He sighed and held his hands out, and when she took them he tugged her forwards so that she crawled onto him. 'Let's stick to what we have in common for the moment.'

'Deal.'

He would change her mind—he had no doubt about it.

Jasmine woke the next morning when the sunlight peeked through the wooden blinds on his window. Pale light filtered through the slats, indicating a rare showing of sun that was uncharacteristic for winter.

She was curled up on her side, Grant's body wrapped protectively around her. The hardness of his thighs pressed under hers, the hairs tickling her skin. One arm was slung over her midsection, heavy and comforting. As the haze of sleep cleared her vision she looked around the room.

She'd never seen a more impersonal sight in her life. It was far neater and more organised than she'd expected, but the distinct lack of personal effects was startling. A memory flickered in Jasmine's mind—something Grant had said last night before they'd argued about her going to the Brownlow with him. He'd once told her that his family life was strained. She'd thought nothing of it at the time— didn't everyone have a little strain in their family life? But she couldn't recall a single instance when he'd mentioned another person other than his coach and his ex-fiancée.

Then there was the lack of photos in his house, and he'd never taken a phone call or a text during their time together. Surely it wasn't possible that someone who was a household name had not a single person to call his friend?

She rolled over, watching as he stirred into wakefulness. A sleepy smile passed over his lips as he blinked, the lure of slumber pulling his eyes closed.

'Good morning.'

'*Very* good morning,' he replied, ducking a hand under the sheets and finding her naked breast.

'You're an animal.' She laughed, swatting away his hand and shrieking when he rolled on top of her.

'I prefer finely tuned athletic machine.'

His grin all but melted her bones, and she could feel him growing excited again.

'Can I be the one to propose coffee this time?' she asked.

'Don't think I'm going to forget about this.' He pushed up, giving her space to wriggle out of the bed. 'I'm dragging you back in here after breakfast.'

'Deal.'

Though her limbs were aching, and the memory of his touch still burned brightly, the thought of coming back to bed with Grant was no less thrilling. She looked around for something to wear. Her leotard and tights were still in a pile where she'd stripped them off last night.

'Here.' He pulled a T-shirt from his drawer and tossed it to her.

Grateful, she slipped the fresh cotton over her head. The hem skimmed the underside of her bottom and the fabric swam around her.

'Now, *that's* a sight to wake up to.'

They wandered out to the lounge room and Jasmine made herself at home on a bar stool while Grant fired up his coffee machine. The scent of freshly brewed coffee filled the apartment, combined with his scent on her skin and the clean cotton of his T-shirt. She was in heaven. Cosy, new relationship heaven.

She frowned. This was *supposed* to be casual. She'd been the one to label it such last night... It felt anything but casual. Could she possibly trust him to see if there was anything more between them? Anything deeper?

Blowing a stray stand of hair out of her eyes, Jasmine pushed the confusing questions from her mind and watched as he moved effortlessly around the kitchen. He made the coffee on a big, fancy machine that had probably cost more than she'd be able to spend on a car.

'So you could afford the swanky apartment but not a decorator?' she asked, accepting a coffee cup and blowing on the steam.

'Ouch.' Grant chuckled. 'You sure know how to hurt a guy's feelings.'

'I only ask because it's so plain. No photos or anything.'

'I have a fruit bowl.' Grant gestured lamely to the single apple that looked lost in the giant metal bowl. 'I don't have any pictures to put up.'

'None at all? No family pictures? None of you goofing around with mates at footy training?'

'I'm a bit camera-shy.' He shrugged.

His face was expressionless but she'd learned to watch out for the tell-tale tightening of his shoulders. He gripped his coffee mug a little too tightly.

'That's sad.'

Silence descended on the kitchen.

'The papers do their best to take lots of photos. I don't need to do it as well.' He took a gulp of his black coffee. 'I get a bit sick of being in the spotlight, to be honest.'

A sad smile played across her lips. 'I don't think I'd ever get sick of the sound of an audience applauding.'

'An audience applauding and the paparazzi harassing you while you're trying to have a night out are two different things.'

'Aren't your family upset when they come here and see you've got no photos of them up?' It was a loaded question, but she couldn't keep herself from wanting to confirm her suspicions.

'Like I said before, our relationship is a bit strained.' He shrugged. 'They've never been here.'

'Never?'

'No.' He shook his head and attempted a smile, but emotion flickered close to the surface. 'My family lives a long way away. It's too far for them to visit.'

'Do you go and visit them?'

'What's with the *Dr Phil* act?' He pushed a few buttons on the coffee machine and filled up another cup.

'I figured since you're so interested in my future with dancing that maybe I could help *you* with something.'

'You have helped me with something.' He blew on the steam curling from his cup. 'My hamstring is in the best shape it's ever been, thanks to you. I might finish the season without injuring it again.'

A satisfied smile curved Jasmine's lips. 'Good. So the next thing you need to work on is the family stuff.'

He didn't need to respond—the guilt on his face was

response enough. She wasn't exactly the best person to offer advice on this kind of thing—she hadn't seen her folks in a while either, but she was planning on mending that, along with making another visit to her physio to see if her ankle had made any progress.

Still, she wrote emails and called her parents once a week, and they knew better than to ask about her injuries. It would take time for her guilt to ease, but at least she was on the right path. Grant, however, was a different story. Her heart clenched for him.

This can't just be casual sex...not with feelings like this.

'Jasmine, I...' He trailed off, looking down to his coffee cup.

'You should call them some time, before it's too late.'

'I wish it were that simple.'

'Isn't it?' They couldn't possibly blame him for what had happened with the court case. 'Surely they know you didn't hit those men?'

'It's not about that.' He shook his head, his eyes focused away from her.

'Talk to me, Grant.'

He hesitated. 'I had a huge fight with them when I left to come to Melbourne to play footy. I never managed to fix it.'

'What was the fight about?'

She waited, biting back the urge to say anything else. It was a trick she'd learned a long time ago: the less you said the more others would want to fill the silence.

'Well, my father wasn't exactly supportive of my decision. He'd always thought I'd go into the family farming and veterinary business. I had the brains to do it but I just wasn't passionate about it.'

'That's fair enough.'

'Not in his eyes.' Grant sighed. 'Mum was always the supportive one—the buffer between Dad and me. After she died and I decided to give footy a go…it all fell apart. He said that I had a choice. I could choose football or my family, but I couldn't have both. My sister was left to pick up the pieces. She gave up her dreams of being a model to stay with Dad and help out with the business. I think she's always blamed me for it.'

'That's not fair.'

'No, it's not.' He shook his head, playing with his coffee cup.

'Did you ever try to make amends after you moved here?'

'Yeah, things were getting better at one stage. I'd reached out to Annabel and she was starting to come around. We were close growing up and she missed me. She'd even started working on Dad—we spoke a few times when he picked up the phone at their office.'

She sensed the 'but' before he had a chance to say it.

'But then everything turned to crap after I started drinking again and those charges made the news. He said I'd dragged the family name through the mud, that I was a bad egg and a poor example to my nephew. Even Annabel turned her back on me. She said she didn't want her son growing up to be like me. She said I'd hurt Dad too many times for her to forgive me.'

When he didn't continue she asked, 'And that was it?'

'Yep. Haven't heard from them in over six months.' He drained his espresso and set the cup down on the bench with a loud clink. 'Country men don't do so well with sharing their feelings.'

'You seem to be doing a good job.'

He gave her a rueful smile. 'I guess that's what happens when you've bottled things up for so long. It has to come out some time.'

'Then maybe your father is feeling exactly the same way,' she pointed out. 'Have you tried calling them?'

'They made it clear they want nothing to do with me.'

The pinch of his brows and the faraway look in his eyes almost broke her in two. His hands were white-knuckled on the edge of the breakfast bar, and there was a slight shake in his grip.

'You should try, Grant. What if something were to happen?'

'I *said* they don't want anything to do with me.'

Jasmine leant over the breakfast bar, almost knocking her coffee over in the process, so she could plant a kiss right on Grant's lips. Somehow she thought it might actually be possible to kiss his problems away.

He met her hungrily, his teeth nipping at her lips as she braced herself against the countertop.

'I'm going to stop this now.' He eased her back gently. 'Otherwise I won't have the will power to leave and get us breakfast.'

'Be quick.' She slid back onto the bar stool. 'Actually, I would love to take a shower.'

'Towels are in the cupboard by my bedroom.' He came around the side of the bench and planted a kiss on her forehead. 'I won't be long.'

When he left the apartment she was engulfed by the silence. What was she *doing*? The whole thing with Grant had spiralled so quickly out of control and now she was here, in his place, feeling far too much as if she wanted to hang around, knowing far too much about who he was. She was thinking things she had no right to be thinking... feeling things she had no right to be feeling...things that indicated something more than what they'd agreed upon.

Abandoning her coffee cup, Jasmine went in search of towels. She found the linen closet in the hallway, where Grant has said it would be. The shelves were stacked with all manner of football equipment—guernseys, footy boots—and there was a single shelf dedicated to towels.

A gold box sat on the lowest shelf, its ribbon sparkling and drawing her eye. Curious, she bent down and slid it from the shelf, her breath catching in her throat when she saw her name in his handwriting. It was light, and the packaging was free of any branding. The box itself was smooth and expensive-looking, with large gold swirls embossed on the thick cardboard.

A small card was tucked into a fold of the ribbon. It read simply: 'Jasmine, come to the Brownlow with me. Grant.' She slipped the lid off and placed it next to her. Inside there was something wrapped in fine apricot tissue paper.

It was a dress—possibly the most divine dress Jasmine had ever seen off a mannequin. She lifted it up, treating it as though it were made of delicate crystal.

It was long—floor-sweepingly long—and made of pale pink silk the exact colour of ballet shoes. The neckline was intricate—a refined tangle of plaited silk and tulle strands embroidered with tiny seed pearls.

For a moment she couldn't breathe. It looked as though a designer had deconstructed a tutu and turned it into an elegant gown. The body itself was plain, simplistic, but the attention to detail in the neckline elevated it to a piece of art.

It was so perfectly *her*.

Jasmine's head pounded. She hadn't even said yes and he'd bought her a dress, given his written command. *Come to the Brownlow with me.*

It was an instruction, not an invitation. There was no question—as though he assumed she could not possibly refuse him. Her cheeks heated as she placed the gown back in the box, folding the tissue paper gently over it, tucking the card neatly back in its place.

She carried the box to the kitchen table, her hands shaking. This was precisely why they couldn't be together—he couldn't take no for an answer. While she was sure his intentions to take her to the Brownlow were good, the fact that he couldn't accept her refusal was *not*.

Whatever this thing was between them, it had to stop. She'd promised herself long ago that she wouldn't be anyone's arm candy. She was done with that. Memories of her accident came flooding back. Her gown had been beautiful that night too. They'd had to cut it from her, and the bloodied silk had ended up in a trash can as a sickening symbol of the life she'd ruined.

She looked around the apartment, her stomach somersaulting as she decided what to do. She knew her feelings for Grant had grown, but it wasn't enough to make her backflip on her promise to herself. If she said yes this time who knew where it would end? It had started out the same way with Kyle, and a little persistence and persuasion had ended with her being a living, breathing trophy.

Grabbing the envelope with her name on it, she flipped it over and borrowed a pen from the kitchen bench. Scrawling a note to Grant, she fought back the rise of bile in her throat. She couldn't go on pretending they had something when she wanted nothing to do with such a large part of his life...the *largest* part of his life.

She had to end it before it had even started.

CHAPTER THIRTEEN

GRANT ROLLED HIS shoulders back and stretched his arms out in front of him. He stood outside the ballet studio, mixed emotions flowing through him hot and fast. The thought of seeing Jasmine was setting him on edge, and he fought the urge to turn around and leave her behind.

He'd raged when he'd come back to find a note telling him she didn't want the dress and she didn't want him. The rejection had stung—not only because he'd thought there was something between them, but because she'd left him in *exactly* the same way as his ex-fiancée.

She had fled by leaving him a note. A goddam *note*. She hadn't even had the guts to say it to his face. Heat flared within him, his fists clenching by his sides. He had to do it—he had to know if this was really the end.

He marched into the ballet studio, channelling all his energy into driving him forwards. This was it. If he couldn't resolve things with Jasmine he was going to swear off women for ever.

The building was deserted, and she was packing her bag in the front room. At the sound of his unceremonious entrance she snapped her head up, eyes opening wide. She sucked in a breath.

'You weren't going to wait for our lesson?' he asked, gesturing to her packed bag.

'I didn't think you'd be coming.' Her voice was steady

but she looked poised to make a break for it—like a spring forced down, ready to release at any second.

'I can't leave things with a note.' He sat down on the couch and folded his hands in front of him. 'I need an explanation.'

'I don't have to explain anything.'

'No, you don't. But tell me you don't think I *deserve* an explanation.'

Silence. She assessed him, her eyes roaming up and down as though she expected him to lash out at her. He didn't want to think about her being so badly treated she couldn't even have a conversation without expecting the worst.

'I promised myself that I wouldn't let another man own me, and I'm sticking to it.' Her face was full of false bravado. 'Now, will you leave me alone?'

'Only if you tell me what the deal-breaker was.'

'You wanted to parade me around at some stupid footy function and when I said I'd think about it you took that as a sign to give me a dress that probably cost more than my entire savings. You can't buy me.'

'I wasn't trying to buy you.' Her accusation settled in his gut. He was *not* that kind of guy.

'Then explain the dress.'

'I wanted you to be my date to the Brownlow. It's one of the most important events in my career and I wanted you by my side.' He couldn't help the wave of emotion that rose within him. He threw his hands up in the air. 'God, so many women would kill to be in your shoes right now.'

He knew it was the wrong thing to say as soon as the words left his mouth.

'Listen to you,' she said, getting to her feet and planting her hands on her hips. 'I'm not *so many women,* Grant. I'm me. And I don't want to go to the Brownlow or any other stupid event. No dress will make me change my mind, and if you can't understand that then I guess it's a good thing we didn't try to make it work between us. Why don't you just take someone else?'

'Judging by the look on your face, I'm going to assume you don't mean that.'

Her brows were pinched, her lips were drawn into a flat line and her skin was lacking its usual lustre.

'I do mean it. This thing—whatever it is—it's over.'

'How can you be such a coward?'

The words scythed through her with an intensity that almost made Jasmine lose her legs. She couldn't believe that he'd arrived here demanding an explanation and then had the audacity to call her names when she didn't comply. It was *exactly* the reason they shouldn't be together. Why, then, did she want to curl up into a ball and cry?

'Coward?' She jabbed a finger in Grant's direction, cheeks aflame and eyes unblinking. 'You have absolutely no right to come here and call me a coward. *You* are the one who can't get up the guts to reconcile things with your father and you call *me* a coward?'

'You don't want to bring my family into this.'

She wondered for a second if his eyes might actually set her ablaze. They were almost electric with fury, but his voice was icy and calm. He rose slowly from the couch, his sheer size dwarfing her by comparison.

'But I do, Grant.' She stuck her chin out. 'You come here to my place of work and call me a coward. Were you expecting me to accept that? You're so goddamn stubborn that you can't even see past your own pain to what really matters. Call your father. You've hurt him as much as he's hurt you. You'd see that if you stopped focusing on yourself for a few seconds.'

She'd hit a nerve. His lips pressed together and he pulled his shoulders back, but she couldn't miss the hurt simmering close to the surface. She wanted to grab his shoulders and shake him until he could see what he was throwing away.

A little voice hinted that she might be doing exactly the same thing, but she pushed it aside.

'That's none of your business,' he said.

'Just like my reason for not wanting to go to the Brownlow is none of yours.'

'You're putting me in the same box as your ex, and I'm not like him. You know that.'

Grant stepped forwards, sending Jasmine's nerves on high alert.

'I'm not trying to use you. I'm not trying to parade you around. I just want to be with you and I know you want to be with me.'

'You want to be with me on *your* terms.' She stepped back, desperate to put distance between them because she could feel herself breaking. 'And that's not good enough for me. I won't change myself to suit you.'

'I'm not asking you to change. I'm asking you to trust me.'

'You're *telling* me.'

His voice was deep and low, his disbelief palpable in the air between them. 'How can you be so frightened of giving us a chance?'

'Because I know what happens when I go against my better judgement.'

As soon as she said it she felt regret seep through her like a poison. Her heart hammered out of control. What had she done?

The barriers shot up around him so quickly Jasmine felt as though a door had been slammed shut in her face. He was slipping away and she was letting it happen.

His nostrils flared as he drew a long, deep breath. 'And being with me is going against your better judgement, is it?'

'Yes.' It was a whisper so powerful it sliced right through the thick, heady air between them.

'Then you're right. There is nothing between us.'

Hearing the words from his mouth was even more painful than hearing them in her own head. Somehow when he said it was over it suddenly felt real. *Over before it had even started...*

'I know I'm right.'

The lie tasted sour in her mouth. She'd never been so uncertain of a decision in her entire life. Her head was pushing her to run, but her heart was already crying out at the loss of him. He was dangerous—she'd known that from the outset—only now she realised just how much he had the ability to split her in two.

The echo of the door slamming behind him seemed to stretch on for ever. Jasmine sat on the ground, wondering if she'd just made the biggest mistake of her life.

Spring had dissolved the chill from the air and there was even a little sunshine peeking through the clouds. The Grand Final was looming and with each passing week the Jaguars inched closer to success.

Painful as it was, Grant put Jasmine out of his mind. it was necessary for both their sakes. Still, her parting words had affected him more than he'd ever admit.

Her swipe about him being too cowardly to make up with his father had caused many a sleepless night, and he'd thought long and hard about his family. About the way he'd grown up, the way he'd been treated, and the way he'd treated his father and sister. He could go on clinging to the bad memories as an excuse not to see them. He could use his father's lack of communication as a shield. Or he could make the first steps in putting it all behind him. His relationship with his father would take work, but it would be worth the effort. He could see that now.

Despite the fact that Grant had not been able to convince Jasmine to give their relationship a chance, he still owed her a lot. Talking to her had lifted a great weight from his shoulders and her comments on his reluctance to make amends had given him a new perspective. It was an angle he'd not been able to see on his own, and since he'd been living as a veritable hermit for the past year she'd been the first person to see past the façade he presented to the outside world.

She'd helped him see that he was as much a party to the problems as his father was. That he'd done some of the hurting along the way.

A deep ache in his chest had started up as he'd left the ballet studio that night, darkening his world until he'd felt that he might not be able to face daylight again. But he had to. This time he wouldn't take the coward's way out. He would face his problems and he *would* rebuild his life.

Step one was contacting his father. He'd tried calling home a few times so far, typing the number into his phone and planning out what to say. Each time he'd chickened out—but he wasn't giving up...not by a long shot.

He typed the number into his phone again and pressed the call button before he could back out. His fingers hovered over the cancel button, but the call was answered on the first ring.

'Hi, Dad. I know it's been a while...'

The desire to dance scratched at her senses, burrowing deep in her skin and prickling at her so she couldn't ignore it. Even after her not-so-successful return at the Winter Performance she couldn't supress the desire. In those moments before she'd fallen the world had made sense. Sure, she'd tried to jump in at the deep end, but watching the playback tape of the concert had shown her that the majority of the audience wouldn't have noticed a thing...

and she'd looked good. She still danced like a pro, even if she couldn't pull her *pointe* shoes out of the closet yet.

She'd started practising in her living room, where no one could see. She'd moved the couch and turned up the music to test out new moves and see how far she could push her ankle. One night it had resulted in a bag of frozen peas being wrapped around her foot, but she'd recovered. Quickly.

She had to keep busy. Sitting around thinking about Grant and dancing was killing her.

Grabbing her coat from the stand in the entranceway, she headed for the front door. As she stepped outside a smile spread across her face. The sun was out and bright light filtered through fluffy clouds. Spring was making its first proper appearance, even though it was nearing the end of September. She tilted her face to the sky, enjoying the mild air as it brushed over her cheeks and nose. It smelled of last night's rain and the orange-blossom tree in her neighbour's yard.

It was the scent of happiness.

As she was about to leave her driveway she noticed the mail sticking out of her letterbox. The handwriting on one letter caught her eye. She'd seen that chicken-scratch scrawl before.

Grant.

Unceremoniously she snatched the letter and tore it open, leaving the edges jagged in her haste. A flyer for a dance company, a business card and a brief handwritten note.

Jasmine,

I've done some research. The director of the Melbourne Contemporary Dance Company is a huge Jaguars fan. I've traded membership for a meeting. Call him to arrange a time.
Grant.

A lump lodged in her throat as she stood rooted to her driveway, a light breeze fluttering the leaflets in her hand. She'd done her utmost not to think about Grant in the weeks since their argument. She'd rationalised away the curling need in her belly and the ache in her chest. She'd talked herself through all of the reasons they couldn't be together, chanting them like a mantra.

Yet he was constantly in her dreams, and in the moments where her concentration slipped and her mind wandered to better times. His touch haunted her; his smile was forever etched into her memory. She couldn't forget how she'd felt with him—how she'd blossomed and come alive again under his kiss. In her weak moments she'd thought about calling him…she'd fantasised about how she could make it better between them. But then she'd wonder what they'd say, and if he'd even be interested in talking to her.

It usually ended with her tucking into a tub of ice cream and then going on a brisk walk to burn the calories.

She missed him. She missed him so badly sometimes that she couldn't sleep for the cavity in her chest that felt as if it would swallow her whole. Being without him was like trying to be half a person. He'd burrowed into her life without her even realising it, and she felt his absence as keenly as she would feel the loss of a dear friend.

Jasmine flipped the envelope over; it was postmarked within the past week. He was still thinking about her. She'd made it clear that there was nothing between them, and yet he'd gone ahead and done something thoughtful for her. Why? Was he hoping the goodwill gesture would win her over?

She bit down on her lip and carried the mail to her room. She tucked the leaflets and his note into her lingerie drawer and closed it with a slam. The note didn't change anything. It didn't change who he was, or his lifestyle. Nor did it change her or her ideals.

She'd made her bed and now she had to lie in it.

* * *

Spring had well and truly arrived in Melbourne, and with the Grand Final less than a week away the city was hoping the weather would hold. Jasmine, on the other hand, had taken to torturing herself with the excessive media coverage of finals fever.

Now she was sitting on her bed, watching the pre-Brownlow hype. In a short while the players and their partners would take to the red carpet for a media feeding frenzy. Would Grant have someone on his arm? Was he even missing her?

God, why did she even care? It was over and it was at her hands. But the thought that he'd be there with someone else was killing her, causing her stomach to tumble around. Clamping her eyes down, she shoved the taunting images from her mind. It was useless. She was miserable without him but she couldn't be *with* him...or at least it had seemed that way at the time.

Next to her bed, the brochure for the Melbourne Contemporary Dance Company was on her nightstand; the director's business card was tucked into her notebook. She'd been putting off making the call, but something was pushing her.

She wanted that feeling: the incredible elation that came from doing something you'd always dreamed of. But she was procrastinating.

First it had been because she'd needed clearance from her doctor. She'd wanted to be doubly sure, so she'd seen her physiotherapist as well...and her old mentor from the Australian Ballet.

She'd then taken her doctor's advice and set up an appointment with someone to help her work through the emotional issues associated with her accident and the sudden end to her career.

Turning the brochure over in her hands, she ran her fingertips across the pictures of the dancers in their modern costumes. It would be a different world, but one where she might be able to relinquish some of the control she so desperately craved. The shrink had said it was a mechanism for her to deal with what she'd lost and the years of emotional abuse inflicted on her in her relationship with her ex. She'd shrugged; there was no way she'd give him the satisfaction of confirming that he was right...though that in itself was telling enough.

Taking a deep breath, she tapped in the number on the business card as quickly as she could before she lost her nerve.

'Hello?' The voice on the other end was rich, cultured.

'Mr Antonio? This is Jasmine Bell. I was given your number by Grant Farley, regarding a meeting with you.'

'Ah, Miss Bell,' he said, his tone lightening with recognition. 'I've been waiting for your call. I was starting to wonder if you hadn't received my number.'

'It's been a busy few weeks. I'm teaching at the moment, and we've started competition season.'

'Yes, Mr Farley has told me all about you. He promised me you would take my breath away. Those are some big words to live up to, my dear.'

'I know.' Butterflies swarmed in her stomach. The kindness of Grant's words was making her insides ache.

'I would love to meet you. We're always on the lookout for new talent, and Mr Farley told me that you were a soloist with the Australian Ballet.'

'That's right.'

'And you can't dance *en pointe* anymore?'

'Yes, sir.'

'We can work with that. Have you been cleared to train?'

'Yes.' By three separate people with more degrees than she could possibly comprehend.

'Perfect. Why don't you come by the office next week? Call my assistant to make an appointment, her number is on my business card.'

'I certainly will.'

'I look forward to meeting you, Miss Bell.'

'You too.'

She stood in the centre of her room, her heart fluttering like a butterfly trapped in a cage. Making sure the call had been disconnected, Jasmine let out a scream. The noise echoed off the walls of her unit as she shook her head and danced about in a circle, expelling her pent-up energy.

Nerves flooded her body. The thought of training and performing again for a living was too much to contain. She let out an exhilarated laugh, and clamped her hands over her mouth.

He promised me you would take my breath away...

The words swirled in her blood, making it rush and pound and sending desire and giddiness all through her. She was turning her life around and it was all thanks to Grant. Without his belief she might not ever have been able to contemplate dancing again. While everyone else had walked on eggshells around her he'd been able to call it as it was. Unbiased honesty—it was perhaps the best gift he could have given her.

God, she missed him. Her gut told her she'd made a huge mistake in pushing him away. He was nothing like Kyle. Her ex had abandoned her instead of encouraging her to dance again. He'd never once opened up about himself the way Grant had that day she'd run away. The memory still stung. The note she'd left him *had* been cowardly. What if she'd stayed to face him? Might they still be together now? Perhaps they would have worked through it... But she'd seen red at the time, with memories clouding her judgement.

She should have stayed.

Grant was exactly the kind of man she wanted in her life and she'd let him go.

Something flickered and caught her eye where she sat. A thin beam of light peeked through her blinds and reflected off something shiny. She walked over to the closet and saw amongst the conservative pants, jeans and long skirts that had become her camouflage that there was a peek of something beautiful.

She pulled out a floor-length gown of indigo silk. It was scalloped at the bottom, and the elegant cowl neck was decorated with the tiniest, most fragile black glass beads.

A few months after she'd quit the Australian Ballet money had been so tight that she'd sold all of the gowns and cocktail dresses that had been her after-hours uniform back in those days. The money had helped her survive a few more months and she'd also cleaned out the items that had embodied her bad memories.

All except this dress. It was the only one she'd bought with her own money, because she'd wanted to wear something of her own choosing. The tiniest of rebellions, but it had meant the world to her at the time.

She held it against her in front of the mirror. The deep-coloured silk made her skin look even more translucent than it usually did. She was white as porcelain by comparison. The heavy silk was like liquid beauty against her palms.

Could she…?

The players would be arriving at the red carpet half an hour from now. If she called a cab she *might* make it.

The face in the mirror was from the past, the hopeful sparkle in her eyes unfamiliar. She bit down on her lip. Her mind was telling her to slow down and think about her actions but for once she pushed her fear aside; it had got her nowhere in the past year except to make her life as lonely as a *pointe* shoe without someone to dance in it.

She grabbed her phone, ordered a cab and stripped on the spot. She was going to get her life back on track, and that meant making new rules.

The dress flowed over her body like a caress, every delicate curve highlighted by the glistening fabric. The neckline sat perfectly, the beads catching the light so that it looked like a piece of night sky.

Outside the cab honked its horn and Jasmine rushed out, teetering on a pair of high heels she'd plucked from the depths of her cupboard. Her hair was loose and it fluttered behind her as she ran.

'To the city, please,' she said breathlessly as she slid into the cab. 'Whiteman street.'

'You know you won't be able to get in there?' the cabbie said, looking at her in the rearview mirror with a look that said *Beware—crazy woman on board*. 'It's the Brownlow tonight.'

'That's where I'm going.'

CHAPTER FOURTEEN

SHE PULLED A mirror from her purse and checked her face. Her cheeks were flushed pink from the cold and the excitement in her eyes made up for a lack of mascara.

'Don't they usually send fancy cars?' The driver eyed her through the rearview mirror. 'Why are you getting a cab?'

'It's a last-minute thing.'

The cab slowed as they approached the city, the traffic thickening and blocking their way. Jasmine bounced in the back seat, nerves settling in now she had nothing to do put ponder what she was going to say to Grant.

What *could* she say? That she'd been wrong to push him away? That he'd helped her trust again?

She sighed. If only she'd known at the time what revealing her scars to him—inside and out—had meant.

What if she said all of those things and he rejected her? A heavy ball of nerves rocked in her stomach, causing her to press her hand against her belly. If he did, she would have to deal with it…but she didn't want to live without trying. She wouldn't allow fear to rule her life anymore.

The cab was now stuck in traffic on Spencer Street. A line of limos rounded the corner several blocks ahead; they would take their turn at dropping the players off at the entrance to the red carpet. How would she even find Grant?

All of the limos were identical—or at least they looked

so from this distance. She would have to check every last one. And then what? What if he had a date with him? Was she going to accost him right in front of the paparazzi?

Her head pounded. She hadn't though the plan out beyond putting on her dress and getting herself into the city. This could very well be a disaster.

But she couldn't stop—not now. Now that she was here...now that he could be around that corner. The very thought of seeing him twisted her stomach into knots. She'd shielded her heart for so long that she didn't know what it was like to be free. What if she'd realised too late?

Exhilaration coursed through her veins as she imagined falling into his arms, pressing her lips to his and telling him that she loved him. *Whoa! Where had that come from?*

As she said those three terrifying words in her head warmth spread through her, thick and sweet and comforting. A weight lifted from her chest and she could breathe again. She took in great mouthfuls of air as the realisation dawned on her.

She loved Grant.

She loved his crooked smile, the bump on his nose, and the way he did things for her even when she didn't want him to. She loved his secret tenderness and the way he made her feel as if she was the only person in the room. She loved the way he accepted her, scars and all.

She loved him.

The cab was chugging along Spencer Street, with the traffic thick and heavy as the limos clogged up the road. Jasmine checked her phone. The first players would already be walking the red carpet.

'I have to get out of here.' She fished in her purse for money to pay the driver.

'But we're not at Whiteman Street, miss.'

'It doesn't matter.'

She threw a twenty over the seat. It was more than

she had to pay, but she couldn't afford to wait for change. Those precious minutes could mean the difference between finding Grant and losing him to the blinding glitter of the red carpet.

Possibly for ever.

She pushed open the door and stepped out of the cab into the wind and cool air. Her hair swirled around her as she ran, and goosebumps rippled across her arms and chest.

The thin straps of her heels bit into her feet as she ran. Stumbling, she turned the corner onto Whiteman Street, to where the limos were lined up. Her heart pounded with adrenaline; her blood pulsed as she searched for him. She bent down to the first one and startled the dark-haired player and his very pregnant partner.

Not here.

She searched the next limo, and the next. Grant was nowhere to be seen.

Staff lined the street: security guards with their don't-mess-with-me expressions and event organisers carrying clipboards.

'Ma'am?'

A woman with an official-looking lanyard approached her. Her brow crinkled. It could have been in concern, though Jasmine suspected that it might have been in wariness. She must look like a crazy person, with her hair in disarray and her dress flowing behind her as she jogged in a pair of most unsuitable shoes.

'Can I help you?'

'I'm looking for Grant Farley.' Her voice would barely work above the thundering of her heart and the heaving of her chest. Nerves had stolen her breath, and the crisp spring air seeped right through her dress, making her shiver. 'He plays for the Jaguars, he should be here.'

'Are you on the guest list?' The woman eyed her suspiciously as she glanced down at the paper on her clipboard.

'Jasmine?'

She turned towards the voice.

Grant hung out of the window of one of the limos, his mouth agape.

'Grant!'

She dashed away from the clipboard lady and towards the black limo. He pushed open the door and stepped out on the street, moving as easily in the inky black tux as he did in his sports gear.

Her heart almost stopped at the sight of him. He suited up well. His thick blond hair was mussed just so; his black bow tie nestled perfectly at his throat. His eyes widened as he drank her in, his gaze smoothing over her dress.

'I thought you didn't do galas.' He shook his head at her.

'I don't.' She stepped forwards, her clutch pressed to her stomach as though the barrier might save her from his rejection.

'I thought you didn't want to be paraded around like a piece of meat?' He stepped closer, so that there was only her bag between them.

Something flickered within the depths of his eyes—something passionate beneath the icy surface of that unwavering blue.

'I don't want that.'

'Then what *do* you want?' His voice was rich but jagged, like silk roughened by stone.

'Dancing,' she said, her voice catching in her throat. 'And dinner…and sex…lots of flexible, mind-blowing sex. I want *you.*'

'You left me without even saying goodbye.' He shook his head, his fingers pressing against his temple. 'You left me a *note.*'

'I know.' She bit down on her lip, pleading with her

body to stop shaking. 'I was trying to protect myself from history repeating itself.'

'You freaked.'

He didn't want to understand. He wanted to be angry. He wanted to protect himself too.

'Yeah, I freaked.'

Her deep brown eyes were wide as saucers. She wasn't wearing a scrap of make-up and her hair was loose and flowing around her shoulders—untamed and just-slept-in. She was a fresh rose among poor imitations.

'Then why are you here?'

'I had to see you.'

Her chest heaved beneath her dress and his heart clenched. How could he trust her? At the first sign of trouble she'd fled.

The thing was, after their conversation he'd decided not to give her the dress—he'd decided to respect her wishes. But he hadn't even had the chance to do the right thing.

He hadn't had the chance to explain.

'I...' He shook his head, disorientated by the emotions that swelled in him. 'I can't do this now.'

'Please don't walk away.'

At that moment his date walked up to them. 'Is everything OK, Grant?'

Jasmine's eyes widened and she looked from him to the tall blonde and back again. He expected her to retreat, to step back and run. His stomach churned. What she did now could very well make or break them.

'Excuse me.' She turned her attention to his date. 'I'm Jasmine.'

The woman looked at Grant with a what-the-hell-is-going-on? expression.

'I am so sorry to interrupt your date, but it's important that you know I love this man. I only realised it today on my way here.' Her face was alight, cheeks pink and eyes sparkling. 'But I love him and I can't let him go. So I hope you haven't got any thoughts about getting serious with him.'

'Jasmine,' Grant said, stifling a smile. 'I'd like you to meet Annabel Farley. My *sister*.'

Her mouth formed a shocked O and she blinked. 'You called them?'

'Yeah, I called them…before it was too late.' He sighed, the fight leaving his body. 'I got some very wise advice recently and I decided to make a few changes.'

'You know, now that you mention it, the family resemblance is quite strong.' She pressed a hand to her forehead, her cheeks reddening to an attractive shade of hot pink.

'I'll give you two some privacy,' Annabel said, skipping off to chat to one of the other football players.

'I'm so sorry.' She shook her head, her mouth opening and closing with a failed explanation.

'So you love me, eh?' he teased.

He had to give it to her: she'd done something gutsy, coming here and laying it all out. 'So what else do you want—apart from the flexible, mind-blowing sex?'

'Commitment,' she said, her eyes glittering as she spoke. 'I will do what I need to do to show you that I'm not going to run again.'

'Does that include red carpets?'

'It might do. It might include photos and media. It will definitely include cheering you on at every single game you play until you retire. It will include me wearing your guernsey around the house.'

'Now, *that* sounds like a sight,' he said.

He hovered in front of her, wanting to kiss her but holding back. Could he trust that she wouldn't change her mind about his lifestyle?

'It includes me trusting you…and it means I have a

meeting with the Melbourne Contemporary Dance Company.'

'You called them?' He wanted to grab her and twirl her around, but he needed to be sure she was serious about them. Because he didn't want to meet her halfway—he wanted them to be all the way in. Together.

'I love you, Grant,' she said, her breathing shallow. 'I didn't want to love you, but I do. You've pushed me since the day we met, you've driven me crazy, and I wouldn't have it any other way.'

He laughed. 'Back at you. You're the most dedicated and *difficult* person I have ever known. You didn't give me special treatment because of who I was when the rest of the world was ready to use me for what they could get. You questioned me, argued with me, and I loved every second of it.'

They stood there as the limos crawled past and curious passers-by watched them in the street. But they might as well have been the only two people in the world for all Jasmine cared.

'But what if you wake up one day and decide you can't handle all of this?' He gestured to the fanfare around them—the flashing of the paparazzi's cameras behind him, the limos, the noise and hustle. 'I can't have you leaving me because it gets too much. If you're in, you're in for good.'

'I'm in.' She shook her head and pressed her lips together in determination. 'I'm in all the way.'

'Well, it's a damn good thing we have an extra seat at our table.' He smiled and reached for her, secretly thanking Don's date for pulling out last minute. 'Because I love you too, Jasmine Bell, even if you *are* as stubborn as a bull.'

He crushed his lips to hers, parting them and delving deep for a long kiss that set her pulse racing. Pleasure, desire and love hummed through her body as if she was conducting enough energy to power them both…and the rest of Melbourne.

Lights popped and flashed around them.

'Grant! Grant!' A journalist stuck his microphone towards them. 'Who's the lucky lady?'

'Don't you mean who's the lucky guy?' He held Jasmine close to him and grinned for the cameras. 'That would be me. I'm the luckiest guy in the world.'

* * * * *